WITCH WAY TO BEAUTY AND THE BEACH

THE WITCH WAY MYSTERIES - BOOK 4

JANE HINCHEY

BP
BAYWOLF PRESS
BAYWOLF PRESS

AUTHOR'S NOTE

Hey there! Welcome to a whirlwind of whimsy and wonder in my Witch Way Mysteries. If you've got a soft spot for the supernatural, you're in for a real treat.

This is your gateway to a world where magic and mystery intertwine. The Witch Way series has now woven its full tale, but the magic doesn't stop here. For news on my latest adventures and stories, don't forget to sign up for my newsletter.

Janehinchey.com/subscribe

Are you ready to conjure up some fun and unravel a few bewitching puzzles? I'll see you on the other side!

xoxo
Jane

ABOUT THIS BOOK

Finding a body washed ashore in Whitefall Cove was not how I wanted to start my day.

I much preferred to face the morning with a hot strong caffeinated beverage, but alas, we can't always have what we want. Out on a morning stroll with my familiar, Archie, I couldn't believe my bad luck when we stumbled upon the body of local teenager Emily Sherman washed up on the beach.

Unable to resist the lure of solving the mystery, I immediately set about finding her killer, but untangling a growing list of suspects isn't as easy as I'd initially thought. With an election looming and Councilman Griffin's nephew caught up in the net, the pressure is on to find out whodunnit and close the case.

Let's not mention working side by side with newly single detective Jackson Ward. Murder, mischief, and mayhem I can take in my stride, but a date with Jackson? That's enough to have my magic sparking in nervous anticipation.

CHAPTER

ONE

"This is all your fault."

"I hope so." Gran grinned in delight as a rainbow cloud of colored marshmallowesque ooze cascaded down the walls of Whitefall Cove town hall. It was an interesting effect. Kinda like dry ice, only wet. And sticky. It hit the floor and curled across the room in a big, globby, wave.

"Gran," I warned, not relishing the prospect of getting the sticky substance off my sandals later.

"Harper Jones." Gran snapped her wand at me, and I shot a foot in the air and hovered there. "You need to lighten up, girl. The kids are having fun and that's all that matters. Look."

I spun to look at the six teenagers gracefully dancing through the air, their wands leaving trails of magic dust as they glided and spun, swirled and swooped. They kept in perfect time, and I watched, transfixed. It was like *Dancing with the Stars*, only with magic.

"You've done a great job," I breathed, my heart warming. "They actually stand a chance of winning."

Gran snorted. "You say that like you're surprised. I have done this before, you know."

"What? Tutor teenagers for the Whitefall Cove talent competition? No. No, you haven't."

Gran cocked her head, seemed to consider my words for a second or two before conceding, "Actually I think you're right. That would make a first."

I sighed at her jab. "Fine. Whatever. But seriously, Gran, you cannot use this marshmallow goop as a special effect. And can you please make it stop? Like now? Before it ruins the town hall and we get a bill for the cleanup?"

Gran rolled her eyes so hard she must have been able to see her brain. Flouncing through the air, wand aloft, she totally ignored me, leaving me suspended above the goop that appeared to be alive and now licking at the soles of my sandals. Fine. I'd do it myself. Unlike Gran, in fact unlike most other witches I knew, I didn't need a wand to use magic. With a snap of my fingers the colorful concoction was gone, and I lowered myself to the floor.

"Spoil sport," Gran called. "Today was meant to be a *full* dress rehearsal!"

"Well, you need to rethink your special effects because your team isn't going to win if you drown the audience in marshmallow," I shouted back.

"Harper is right, Mrs. B." Jacob Griffin, one of the teenagers looking very handsome and dashing in a tuxedo, spoke up. He looked more man than boy, easily six foot tall, broad shoulders, yet a gleam in his eye as his gaze landed on his partner, Emily Sherman.

All mischievous youth, Emily, seventeen this summer, glided through the air in her sky blue gown, her blonde hair coiled in artful disarray on top of her head, her laugh easy as she linked hands with Jacob. "We might lose points for that."

Gran threw up her hands. "Okay, fine. Let's change it to pixie dust. Would that make everyone happy?" And then she farted. A little toot that propelled her through the air and set her students into fits of giggles.

I couldn't contain my snort of laughter. "You should incorporate that into your routine," I said.

"I still think Emily and I should swap dresses, Mrs. B!" Sarah McClain looked Emily up and down before flicking her hair over her shoulder. "This one's a bit loose on me and Emily looks like she's about to burst out of hers."

I glanced from Sarah's yellow dress to Emily's blue one. If it weren't for the color, they were identical. Emily snapped her eyes to Sarah, then ran her hands suggestively over her curves. "Feels just fine to me," she drawled, pulling her shoulders back and thrusting out her chest. Jacob's eyes were glued to her cleavage.

"What do you think, babes?" Emily purred, running her hand up his chest. He swallowed, sweat beading his brow.

"You look great in that dress, but I'm betting you'd look even better out of it," was his suave response.

I looked at Gran in surprise. I'd been expecting a bunch of pimply teenagers who were barely out of childhood, but these fully developed youths before me were young adults and the pheromone level in the town hall was so thick I could choke on it.

Sarah gave them a stone cold eye roll and turned her back, flouncing toward her respective partner, Ryan, who was smiling widely at the exchange.

"Aren't I man enough for you, Sarah?" he teased, winking at her.

She patted his arm, swanning past him. "In your dreams, sugar."

"Always." Spinning on his heel, he followed. Sarah preened her hair, pleased with the attention, a ribbon the exact color of her dress adding dramatic effect amongst her chestnut locks.

"Are we taking a break, Mrs. B?" The third girl in the group, Hannah Burton, approached, her own dress a vibrant shade of lavender.

Her dance partner, Ethan, crossed to Jacob and

slapped him on the shoulder with a laugh. "Lucky dog."

"Ten minute break!" Gran called.

Hannah practically sagged in relief, and I watched as she walked away, head down, shoulders slumped. Ethan ignored her, joining his buddies.

"Hannah!" Emily called, "Weren't you going to fix my hair? These pins just aren't holding." Emily was fussing with her hair, which looked pretty darn amazing to me.

Hannah stopped, her back snapping ramrod straight before she turned, face tight. "You're right. Sorry. I mess everything up." She hurried over to Emily and fussed with her hair, that, in my opinion, didn't need fixing at all.

My phone vibrated in my back pocket, dragging my attention from the teenage dynamics playing out before me. Pulling it out, I saw a message from Jenna on the screen.

"*Coffee?*" she wrote.

"*Yes! Bean me up in 5,*" I replied. "See you later, guys. Keep up the good work. You all look fantastic." With a wave, I headed out of the town hall and out onto the main street of Whitefall Cove. Summer was upon us and with it came the tourists. Not that I minded, it meant more business for my bookstore, The Dusty Attic, and a lot more activities that kept Gran out of trouble.

Who was I kidding? She got into more mischief than ever. Take yesterday's sandcastle competition. Her anatomically incorrect rendition of Michelangelo's *David* had been quickly destroyed by the judges and her entry disqualified. And there had been complaints that her G-string was not appropriate beachwear for a family friendly event.

Shaking my head, I wove my way along the sidewalk, my sundress swishing around my legs, the bright red of my toenails peeping through my sandals. For the first time in a long time I felt happy. Content. I had everything I needed. A bookstore that made me happy and indulged my obsession with books; I had a gorgeous home on the bluff overlooking the lighthouse; I had my cat, Archie, and my best friends Jenna and Monica, not to mention Gran. Who cared that I'd gone from having two potential romantic suitors, to zero? I didn't need a man to make me happy. I ignored the niggling little voice in the back of my head that taunted, "Liar."

Reaching Bean Me Up, I spotted Jenna at a table by the window and joined her.

"You look..." Jenna's eyes scoured me from top to toe. "You're glowing!"

"Is that an accusation?" I grinned, sliding into the chair opposite her.

"Absolutely not. You look fantastic, Harper."

"Thank you. So do you. Is that dress new?" Jenna

was in a blue and white polka dot dress that cinched around her waist with a wide black belt.

She looked down at herself then back at me, shaking her blond head. "Nuh-uh, you don't deflect that easily, young lady. Spill. What's got you all glowing?" She tapped her fingers to her chin in thought, then snapped them in triumph. "It's gotta be one Detective Jackson Ward."

I shook my head. "Nope. This happy face before you is the result of fresh air and sunshine. I'm off men—who needs them?" I declared, half meaning it. My friendship with Jackson had always been a little out of the ordinary. When I first returned home to Whitefall Cove nursing a broken heart, I was taken by Jackson's good looks and kind nature. But he was dating a co-worker, police officer Liliana Miles. So my crush on him went unrequited and life continued on.

It wasn't until the tall, dark, and very handsome bad boy lawyer Blake Tennant arrived on the scene, turning my head with his attentions, I'd decided a relationship with Jackson would never be on the cards and maybe a dalliance with Blake was exactly what my bruised heart needed to heal the wound my cheating ex-fiancé had inflicted upon it.

My bad luck with my romantic choices continued its streak. Things with Blake turned out to be a bust. He'd traveled to Australia with me, Gran, and Jenna, when my parents were missing and just when I thought our budding romance would grow, it stalled. He pulled back and as soon as my parents were found safe and well, he'd bailed, leaving without saying goodbye. That was weeks ago, and aside from a bouquet and an apology note delivered upon my return to Whitefall Cove, I'd not heard from him.

"You're thinking about him again." Jenna touched my wrist, dragging me from my thoughts. "Blake."

I sighed. "I guess I'll never understand men," I said.

"They are puzzling creatures," she agreed, playing with the sugar shaker on the table.

"Anything more from Mick? You said last time you spoke with him he wanted to pursue a long-distance relationship?" Mick was Senior Sergeant Mick Gould of Arrowstrand Police Station and he and Jenna had developed a romance during our time in Australia.

"We're trying, but Australia is like another world away. It's not like I can hop on a plane and be there in a couple of hours. It's a twelve hour—if not longer— plane ride, then another six hours by car. And it's expensive." The light in her eyes dimmed, and I clasped her hand on the tabletop. I didn't have any words that would make things easier for her. All I could do was to be here for her and support her in whatever way I could.

"Your articles have been a hit," I said, trying to find a positive to focus on. Jenna had been releasing a new story every week on our adventures in Australia, and her first piece on the murders in Arrowstrand had earned her an award.

She brightened. "My editor is over the moon. Sales are on the up, and with the summer tourist season upon us, the *Whitefall Cove Tribune* is selling out every week."

"That is fantastic!"

"Here we go, ladies." I sat back to make room as the waitress set two iced teas in front of us.

"Thanks, Janet," Jenna said.

"I just saw Ryan at rehearsal," I said to her. "They all look amazing."

Janet beamed with pride. "He's been so excited for this. When we went for the tux fitting, I can't lie, I had a tear in my eye."

"His partner is Sarah, isn't it?" I asked, remembering the girl who'd wanted to switch dresses.

Janet nodded. "Your Gran has been such a godsend for those kids. I was worried about what they'd get up to during the school break, but she's kept them busy with so many rehearsals and other activities to boost their coordination and fitness they've been too exhausted to get into any trouble."

I blinked. Poor Janet. She had no idea. "Good, I'm glad."

Janet gave us a quick smile before hurrying back to the counter.

"Janet's right," Jenna said. "I remember last summer Ryan and his posse got caught egging people's houses. So glad that hasn't happened this year."

I nodded. "Bored teenagers. Do you remember what we used to get up to?"

She snorted. "Smoking, drinking, and sunbathing mostly."

"Sneaking out at night to hang out with Monica." I laughed. "I spent most of my seventeenth summer in a state of exhaustion from lack of sleep."

"The Whitefall Cove talent show will be worth seeing this year," Jenna said, fiddling with her phone.

"Sure is. First time Gran's put up a dance team. And I was serious, they looked amazing. The dance moves are out of this world. As long as Gran keeps the special effects under control." I told her about the lava marshmallow effect I'd walked in on.

"The kids that Gran has taken on, are they all witches?" Jenna asked.

"Sort of. Like me, they're not full bloods and their parents are mostly non-practicing."

Jenna nodded. "They're the underdogs."

"Yeah, I guess. They have some magical ability and Gran has been helping them to develop that in a more fun setting, outside a classroom."

"What does Drixworths think of that?" Drixworths Academy of Witchcraft and Wizardry was where you went to learn the craft and get your witches license. Whitefall Cove had a high population of witches, but we also had our fair share of fae, shifters, and vampires too.

"They're happy for Gran to provide some extra-curricular activities for the students on the proviso they get final approval on the routine. Gran was running them through a dress rehearsal today and I think they're presenting to Izzy tomorrow." Izzy, full name Esmerelda Higginbottom, was headmistress of Drixworths and a friend. She helped me get my witches license back after it was suspended and harness my own magic, which was powerful and out of control.

Finishing my iced tea, I looked at Jenna. "Ready?" We'd promised Wendy, my assistant in the bookstore, that we'd drop by for a visit. She'd recently given birth to a bouncing bundle of joy, Zachariah Sims, and was already going stir crazy being at home with a baby twenty-four seven.

Jenna stood, wriggling her phone in the air. "Let's do this, I foresee a million baby photos in your future."

"*Mroooow.*"

    I cracked open an eye and glanced at my orange cat, Archie, who was sitting on the pillow next to my head, paw raised. "Don't even think about it." I grumbled.

"*Meow.*" The paw dropped, and he cocked his head in that way that is too adorable to resist. I sighed, lifted my head to peer past him to the clock.

"Archie," I whined, "it's not even six."

"*Meooooow.*" His paw landed on my nose with a gentle pat. Throwing back the covers, I slid my legs out of bed. One thing was for sure, this cat had me trained well. Throwing on a robe, I tied it around my waist and used the bathroom before heading downstairs, Archie preceding me with his tail in the air. He sat by his food bowl. His non-empty food bowl.

"You still have kibble, Archie," I grumbled. Nevertheless, I opened an overhead cupboard and pulled out the container holding the kibble and scooped some into his bowl. His face was buried in the bowl within seconds, his purr as loud as the crunching of the biscuits between his teeth. Putting on a pot of coffee, I stood, arms wrapped around my waist, gazing out of the kitchen window toward the lighthouse on the bluff.

I loved it here in the caretaker's cottage. It was quiet and peaceful, and I got to gaze at the lighthouse any time of the day or night. Tours had started now that the weather was warmer, but the extra foot traffic didn't bother me. Some days I'd sit on the front porch and get as much enjoyment from people watching as I did from lighthouse watching.

Archie and I had settled into a summer routine. Up early, breakfast, then a walk along the beach before work. Today was no different. After changing into shorts and a tank, I headed out. We had our own path from the bluff down to the beach and Archie streaked ahead of me, stopping to sniff amongst the bushes, sometimes capturing a stray leaf and carting it all the way to the beach as if he were a great hunter with his prey.

Stepping from the compacted path onto the soft sand, I eased my shoes off and carried them, loving the feel of the sand between my toes. Waves lapped at the shore and Archie played catch me if you can with them, jumping high in the air if the water so much as touched a toe.

"Don't like the surf, huh, boy?" I teased, watching as he scampered up the beach, out of the reach of the encroaching tide. In Australia Archie had loved the water, would happily swim in the watering hole at the place we were staying, but I suspected that had something to do with his canine companion, Bandit, and trying to emulate a dog, rather than an overwhelming love of water.

Although, watching now as he scampered further up the beach and disappeared from view among the colorful beach huts, maybe Archie had a little canine DNA in him after all. At a more leisurely pace I strolled along the shoreline, letting the water lap around my ankles as it surged forward, then retreated. The little wooden beach huts with their alternating jewel colors added a colorful backdrop to my scenic walk. I remembered wanting one of the cabins so badly as a child, harassing mom and dad, who'd argued that we had no need for such a fancy cabana. I admit, the miniature houses with their little gabled roofs and front decks, alternating from green, blue, orange, and yellow, were only really useful to change into your bathing suit, maybe store beach chairs and coolers.

I'd bent to scoop up a shell the tide had washed ashore when Archie's mournful meows alerted me something was up. Squinting, I raised a hand to block out the early morning glare and spotted Archie further up the beach near a lump of seaweed.

"It's okay, Archie," I called, picking up my pace. "It's just seaweed. Nothing to be scared of."

He trotted toward me, stopped, then trotted back to the seaweed and meowed, long and loud. Recognizing the tone of his howl, I broke into a jog, arriving at the lump of seaweed out of breath. Only it wasn't just seaweed at my feet.

"Oh, no," I whispered, reaching down with trembling fingers to brush away the strands of seaweed covering the face of a girl, her skin as white as white, her eyes open and cloudy. "Not again." I sank to my knees beside her body. Archie head bumped my elbow and leaned into my side. Absently I pet him. "It's Emily," I said. Emily who I'd seen dancing just the day before in her beautiful blue dress. Only now she was in sodden jeans and a T-shirt, her body lifeless.

Pulling out my phone, I dialed.

"Harper." Jackson sounded surprised. "You're up early."

"There's a dead body on the beach," I said without preamble.

"What? Do you know who?" His voice changed immediately, as I knew it would. He'd switched from friend mode to cop mode.

"Emily Sherman," I said. "It looks like she drowned."

"I'll be right there. Don't touch anything."

I opened my mouth to reply, but there was nothing but the dial tone humming in my ear. Sliding my phone back into my pocket, I leaned back on my heels and examined Emily. Her skin was deathly white, but around her neck, an ugly purple bruise. Had someone strangled her and dumped her body in the water? She was fully clothed, so however she'd found her way into the water it hadn't been intentional.

The more I looked at her the more I believed that Emily had met with foul play. Quickly pulling out my phone, I took photos of her body. Jackson wouldn't approve, but how could I not try to find out what had happened to the poor girl? It was hard to fathom mere hours ago she was full qf vivacious life, flirting with her boyfriend.

I heard a car screech to a halt and turned to watch as Jackson slammed the door of his car, then made his way across the beach to me. We were at the far end of the cove, the opposite end to the lighthouse, away from the bathing huts. Isolated. Was this where she died? Or was this merely where she'd washed ashore after being dumped at sea?

Jackson strode right up to me, into my personal space, and his hands clamped my shoulders. "Are you all right?" His concern was comforting, as was the warm emerald green of his eyes. I nodded. "I'm fine. I wish I could say the same for Emily."

"You found her like this?" He moved around me to examine the body.

"Archie did," I told him. "I thought it was just a lump of seaweed until I got closer. I cleared the seaweed from her face. Other than that, I haven't touched a thing."

He shot me a look before turning his attention back to Emily's body.

"Bruising around the throat," he said, using a pen to push strands of Emily's hair away from her neck. "Fully clothed." He glanced around. "No sign of a bag or purse."

I watched and waited as he continued his preliminary sweep. In the distance I heard sirens.

"I called them after you called me," Jackson said by way of explanation. I shrugged. I guess I should have called the police station directly, but my first instinct had been to call Jackson. And let's not ignore the fact I was keen to avoid contact with Police Officer Liliana Miles. Our relationship had always been frosty, but now that she and Jackson had broken up it was downright glacial.

Archie wove around my ankles and I bent to scoop him up into my arms, hugging him close to my chest and burrowing my face in his fur. All the while my mind was going over who could have killed Emily. And why? Turning my back on the scene, I gazed out over the ocean, calm today, the sun reflecting off the water, not a boat in sight. The wharf sat empty except for a lone sailing yacht. Given that the water was calm and the air still, I'd imagine whoever owned the yacht wouldn't be sailing until there was a breeze to fill the sails.

"Jones," Liliana said, her voice cold and curt. "Should have known."

I turned to face her, squeezing Archie a little too tight, so he squeaked in protest. "Sorry boy." I put him down and folded my arms across my chest.

"Officer Miles." I nodded in greeting, knowing not to address her as Liliana. I'd made that mistake once and had been told in no uncertain terms never to do so again. I also knew not to volunteer information to her; she had a strict *don't speak to me unless spoken to* policy.

Jackson straightened from his examination of the body. "Good, you're here," he said to Liliana. "Secure the scene."

"What are you thinking?" Liliana asked. "Suicide?"

"Not with those bruises." He pointed to Emily's neck and Liliana leaned in for a better look. "She's got something in her hair." I watched as Liliana and Jackson squatted on either side of Emily and carefully turned her head. Using his pen, Jackson lifted strands of Emily's hair just behind her ear.

"Looks like blood."

I moved to get a closer look and Liliana shot me a look that had me freezing on the spot, a shiver shooting up my spine. She blamed me for the breakdown of her relationship with Jackson, although we weren't seeing each other.

"We've got it from here Jones," she snapped.

Jackson's head whipped up, looking from me to Liliana and back again. "Actually," he drawled, voice soft but holding a hint of steel, "We need her statement. She discovered the body."

"Of course she did," Liliana muttered beneath her breath. She straightened and with a huff pulled out her phone. "Tell me what happened." She hit record, and I dutifully recounted the events of the morning.

Liliana looked from me, to the lighthouse on the bluff. "You get a pretty good view of the beach from up there."

I nodded. "I get a pretty good view of the entire town from up there."

"And you didn't see or hear anything last night?"

I frowned at her. Was she serious? Of course not. The beach wasn't lit at night and unless I stood on my front porch with binoculars, I'd see diddly squat on what went on at the beach. I knew better than to say that. "No," I said instead. I had sat on my porch last night with a glass of red wine and watched the twinkling lights the town, but I hadn't stayed outside for long. Archie and I had a long-standing date

20

to watch Agatha Christie movies on Wednesday evenings.

"You can go." Hitting the screen of her phone, she ended the recording and slid the phone into her police vest pocket. I glanced at Jackson who gave me a slight nod.

"I'll catch up with you later," he said.

"Okay." I hesitated, my heart hurting for the poor girl dead in the sand. "You'll tell Emily's grandmother?"

"We'll inform her family," Liliana said. I hesitated a second, debating whether it was worth telling them what I knew of Emily's family or if I'd get scolded for interfering. Who was I kidding? I wasn't scared of Liliana. Wary, yes. But not scared.

"Emily lived with her grandmother," I explained, keeping my eyes on Jackson and ignoring Liliana completely. "Rose Sherman out on Rigby Road. Emily's parents died when she was a little girl and she's been living with Rose ever since."

Jackson frowned. "Right."

"How do you know that?" Liliana snapped.

Lifting my shoulders in a shrug I said, "I've lived here my entire life—except for the last five years—and I know most everyone who lives here. Philip and Kelly Sherman were killed in a car accident. Emily would have been around nine or ten years old at the time. Just..." I paused, sucking in a breath. "Just be gentle with Rose, okay? She's already buried her son and daughter-in-law. Now she's having to bury her granddaughter too. That's a lot for a person."

Jackson reached out and ran a hand up and down my arm in a soothing gesture. "Thank you."

I nodded, clamping my lips tight against the surge of emotion threatening to overwhelm me. Poor Emily. Poor Rose. It was so sad.

"Okay, well... good luck," I said, digging my hands into my pockets and turning away, beginning the trek back up the beach. "Archie!" I called when I realized he'd disappeared yet again. A muffled meow sounded from the bathing huts before I spotted an orange head poking around the corner of a bright blue hut.

"Come on boy, we're going to be late."

CHAPTER
THREE

"Sorry to keep you waiting, Jordan." Unlocking the door to The Dusty Attic, I stood aside to let Jordan enter ahead of me. "I got held up."

"That's okay. I haven't been waiting long."

Jordan Ray was seventeen and helping in the store over the summer holidays while Wendy was on maternity leave. Jordan reminded me a lot of myself at that age—a socially awkward book nerd.

I locked the door behind us, leaving the small sign hanging in the glass pane to closed. "Something's happened that you're going to hear about, and I think it might be better if you heard it from me first."

Jordan shoved her bag under the desk we used as a counter and turned to smile at me. "Oh?"

"It's about Emily Sherman." I paused. There was

no easy way to say this so I simply said it. "I'm afraid she's dead."

Jordan plopped into the chair, then ran a hand through her straight bob, messing the strands. "Oh."

"Were you friends with her?" I asked sympathetically, crossing to put on a pot of coffee. I'd have offered Jordan a hug, but she didn't like physical contact and the only person she allowed in her personal space was my cat. Sensing his presence was required, Archie jumped up onto the desk and rubbed his head against Jordan's shoulder. Absently she patted him.

"Not really. Emily, Hannah, and Sarah were pretty tight. But I had a couple of classes with her." Her eyes lost their blank expression and focused on Archie.

"I'll understand if you can't work today," I told her. "Take the day off if you need to."

Jordan shook her head. "No. I mean... it's a shock, and it's sad, but... I'm okay. I'd rather work. If that's okay?"

I smiled. "Of course it's okay. If you need to talk, if you need anything, I'm here."

"Thank you, Miss. Jones."

"It's Harper, remember?"

She grinned, showing the braces on her teeth. "Harper. I'll open up then?" She nodded toward the still-locked front door.

"Go ahead."

As predicted, word spread like wildfire about Emily's death. Many of Jordan's classmates stopped by the store to chat and I kept a close eye on the teenager to make sure she was okay. Grief could sneak up on a person, and it affected us all differently.

Gran arrived midmorning, her eyes dull despite the brightly colored muumuu she wore. I shoved a cup of coffee in her hand and led her to the armchair in the reading corner of the store.

"Sit."

She did, without hesitation, even took a sip of the coffee I'd prepared and didn't pull a face or tell me how disgusting it was. Which only went to show how much Emily's unexpected demise had affected her.

"Are you okay?" Perching on the arm of her chair, I slung an arm around her shoulders and squeezed.

"It's such a shame, you know?" Gran's voice wobbled, and I gave her another squeeze. "Don't get me wrong, Emily was quite the diva, definitely the queen bee in her trio of friends, but she was actually getting good with her magic. Quite skilled. Such a shame."

"It's very sad," I agreed. "Do you know her grandmother, Rose?"

Gran snorted. "Child, I know everyone."

I chuckled. "Yes, I know you do, but I mean... do you know Rose well? Are you close?"

Gran was already shaking her gray head. "Nope.

Rose is human, as was her son, Philip. It was Philip's wife, Kelly, who was the witch and passed her magic on to Emily. Such a tragedy when the two of them died. I'm just grateful Rose didn't force her granddaughter to give up that part of her heritage. Although, Lord only knows she needed to rein that girl in, the way she walked all over everyone, determined to get her own way in everything."

We lapsed into silence for a moment, each lost in our own thoughts until Gran straightened her spine, handed me her coffee and said, "Thanks for the swill. If that doesn't revive the dead I don't know what will."

I laughed. Gran had very specific coffee tastes, and I'd learned not to take offense.

"Is it true? You found the body?" she asked me.

"Archie did. On our morning walk along the beach."

"What do you think? Did she kill herself?"

I gasped in shock. "What? Absolutely not! Is that what they're saying?"

Jordan overheard us and came over. "Most of the kids from school are saying she killed herself."

"Why would they think that?" Was it because she was a teenager? That was hardly justification she'd taken her own life.

Jordan shrugged. "Something had been up with Emily for a while."

"Like what?" I pounced.

"Well, she got fired from her job at Silent Bite a couple of weeks ago." Silent Bite was the local fast-food restaurant and predominately hired school students to keep staffing costs down.

"Do you know why?" I asked.

"I think she kept turning up late for shifts? I'm not really sure." Jordan tucked her hair behind her ear where it stayed put for precisely two seconds before swinging forward again.

"She was dating Jacob. Maybe he was keeping her out late," Gran said.

"But her grandmother wouldn't allow that, surely," I said.

Jordan shrugged. "Emily pretty much did what she wanted, when she wanted. I know she and her grandma had been fighting a bit lately—Emily's been bitchier than usual too, really mean and snappy with everyone."

I remembered when I was that age, hormones raging. It had been Whitney who'd been the mega bitch in my class; she was mean and a bully and I'd been on the receiving end more than once. I didn't miss those days.

"You're saying she didn't kill herself?" Gran jolted me out of my thoughts.

I shook my head. "I'm positive she didn't kill herself. She had bruises on her neck, and blood in her hair."

Jordan gasped, and I cursed myself for revealing that in front of her, but I needn't have worried, for Jordan clasped my wrist and said with great eagerness. "Are you going to investigate her murder? Are you going to catch another killer?"

Slowly I nodded. Looked like my murder club was back in business.

With an uncanny sense of timing, my phone rang. It was Jenna.

"Don't tell me," I answered. "You want the scoop."

"Well, of course, but that isn't why I'm calling."

"Oh. Okay, what's up?"

"Word on the street is that Emily Sherman committed suicide. I wanted to know what you thought. You saw the body, what do you think?"

"We were just talking about this." I looked from Gran to Jordan, who were watching me with eager faces. "Let's meet up tonight to discuss."

I could hear the smile in Jenna's voice. "I'll be there the minute you close. I'll let Monica know. And I'll bring pizza."

True to her word, as soon as I flicked the sign on the front door to closed at the end of the day, Jenna appeared, pizza box in hand. With a grin I flicked the snib on the lock and held the door for her.

"Monica is right behind me," she said, stepping inside. I felt my hair lift in a gust of wind as Monica whipped past and into the store. As a vampire she couldn't tolerate a lot of sunlight, and despite it being five thirty, the sun still packed a punch even though it was low on the horizon. She couldn't afford to dilly dally unless she wanted a nasty UV burn.

"Oh." Jenna halted when she caught sight of Jordan. "Hi, Jordan, you're still here." She looked at me quizzically and I shrugged.

"Jordan's keen to help," I explained. "And she may have some valuable insight, given that she went to school with Emily."

Monica unwrapped herself from the scarf she used to cover the lower half of her face, removed the wide-brimmed hat and sunglasses and tossed them onto the counter next to the coffee machine. Despite running the gauntlet of daylight, she looked stunning as always with her alabaster skin and jet-black hair.

"So long as she knows not to breathe a word of this outside this room." Monica pinned Jordan with a hard look and Jordan audibly swallowed while shaking her head. "Oh, I won't. I promise!"

"Pft," Gran snorted, rousing herself from where she'd been dozing in the armchair. "That's easily fixed." Whipping out her wand she aimed it at Jordan and muttered something under her breath before putting the wand away.

"What did you do, Mrs. B?" Monica asked, one dark brow perfectly arched.

"Silencing spell. Even if she wanted to, she can't tell anyone about any of this."

I sighed. "Gran, you really shouldn't be putting spells on people without warning them first. But it's done now. Sorry, Jordan."

Jordan shrugged. "It's okay. I don't mind."

"Right. Now that that's settled." Jenna set down the pizza, flipped the lid open, helping herself to a slice, "I'm starving. Come on, guys, dig in. And, Harper, move your shelves, will you. We need to get the murder board happening."

I whispered the spell that would magically reveal a pinup board we'd affectionately nicknamed the murder board, then helped myself to pizza, dodging Archie's paw as he tried to snag it out of my hand. "Dude, you've got your own food in your bowl."

"You guys eat; I'll get this started," Monica said, opening the top drawer of the desk and pulling out the Post-it notes. Holding a marker aloft, she asked, "Who have we got in our pool of suspects?"

Everyone remained silent. Oh my God, we had no one! We knew nothing of Emily's last movements, who she'd seen last, what she'd been doing.

"Gran, what time did rehearsal finish up yesterday?" I asked.

"Just after you left," Gran replied, mouth full of pizza. "The kids were going to grab a shake at Silent Bite, I think."

"But, Jordan, didn't you say they fired Emily from Silent Bite?"

Jordan nodded. "She was fired."

"So maybe the others went, but Emily didn't?" Jenna said, but Jordan was already shaking her head. "No way. Hannah and Sarah wouldn't have gone off to have milk shakes without Emily. And I doubt Jacob would have left his girlfriend behind."

"What about the other boys... Ethan and Ryan? Were they dating their respective dance partners?"

"I can answer that," Gran said. "And the answer is no. From the googly eyes Sarah kept giving Jacob when she thought no one was looking I'd say that girl was looking to cut her best friend's grass."

"Wait, you're saying Sarah wants to hook up with Jacob?" I asked.

Gran shrugged. "I'm just telling it the way I saw it. And Sarah took every opportunity to get up close and personal with Jacob, brushing up against him as she went past, that type of thing."

"But she's Emily's best friend." Jenna frowned. "You wouldn't try to steal your best friend's boyfriend."

"Not everyone has your moral code, babe," Monica drawled, giving us a wink and a sultry smile.

"I think Mrs. B might be right," Jordan mumbled, chewing on her lip. "Now that I think about it, Sarah touches Jacob a lot. Like on his arm and stuff. And laughs at his lame jokes when no one else does."

Monica wrote Sarah's name down and pinned it to the murder board.

"Wait a minute." Jenna paced. "Whoever killed her had to be strong enough to A, get her into the water, and B, hold her under long enough to drown her. Do we think Sarah is strong enough to do that?"

I remembered the photo I'd taken of Emily's body and swiped through my phone until I had the image on screen. "Here. Look at this. I don't think she drowned. I think someone strangled her." I showed them the bruises on Emily's neck.

Jenna snatched the phone from me and peered at it, manipulating the image with her fingers to increase the size. "I think you're right. But that mark doesn't look like handprints, it's too uniform. It looks like someone tied something around her throat. Do you think Jackson knows the official cause of death yet?" Handing me back my phone, she pulled out her own and dialed, huffing in exasperation when Jackson didn't pick up. Before I could stop her, she snatched my phone from my hands and dialed again.

"Hey." Jackson answered on the first ring.

"Do you know how Emily died?" Jenna asked without preamble.

There was a pause. "Jenna what are you doing with Harper's phone?"

"How did you know it was me?" Jenna shot back.

I could imagine Jackson rolling his eyes. "Because you're a reporter, her best friend, and she's embroiled in yet another murder. Who else would it be? Plus, I recognized your voice."

"Fair point," Jenna conceded.

"Put her on."

With an over dramatic sigh, Jenna handed the phone out to me as if we all hadn't just heard the exchange. "He wants to speak to you."

Accepting the phone, I held it to my ear. "Hi."

"Do I take it that the murder club is in session?" he drawled.

"Possibly." I hedged.

"Most definitely." He chuckled. "I'll come down."

"No!" I shot back. Because if Jackson were here, and I was here, then the ghost of Whitney Sims would appear.

Jackson laughed. "You are such a scaredy cat."

"Yes, well..." I adjusted the neckline of my dress. "It doesn't hurt to be cautious. Now and then."

"You? Cautious? Now I've heard it all." He snorted, then sobered, "Okay look, the autopsy results aren't in yet, so nothing official, but it looks like she was the victim of a stun attack—hit on the back of the head with a blunt object to incapacitate her—and then strangled. But," he warned, "that's not official. And it is off the record."

My eyes shot to Jenna who had moved to stand next to me, her head pressed close to mine so she could eavesdrop on our conversation. She mimed zipping her lips.

"Of course. We won't say a word," I assured him. "So you think someone dumped her body in the water as a means of disposal? That she didn't drown?"

"Possibly. We need to wait for the autopsy results to see if there's water in her lungs. But tossing her into the ocean to get rid of her body was a poorly thought out move. They should have weighed her down. Instead, she washed right up on the shore."

After the call with Jackson I leaned back against the desk, arms crossed, and thought out loud. "Whoever it was had to be strong."

"Not necessarily," Monica argued. "Jackson said a blitz attack. How easy would it be for me to come up behind you and whack you over the head with a rock? Boom. You're out cold on the ground, but not dead. Maybe that had been my intent, to kill you with one blow, but that didn't work, so now I must resort to Plan B. I strangle you. You're unconscious; you're not fighting me at all. I just wrap my scarf around your throat and pull it tight until you stop breathing. And any one of us here in this room would have the strength to do that." I eyeballed the cotton scarf Monica had tossed onto the counter earlier.

"True," Jenna agreed, "but you're forgetting one

thing. Whoever it was then had to dispose of the body, and Emily is the size of an adult woman. And a deadweight. Say I killed her, I'd struggle to move the body after the deed."

"Maybe there were two of them?" Jordan mumbled, and we all looked at her in surprise. She could be right, it was possible more than one person was involved in the death of Emily Sherman.

"Monica, put all the names up. Something happened yesterday to trigger the murderer into killing her."

"Hit me with the names," Monica said, Post-it notes in hand.

"Sarah McClain, one of Emily's best friends. And Hannah Burton, her other best friend," I said.

"Jacob Griffin, her boyfriend," Gran added, "and Ethan Moss and Ryan Noble, the other members of the dance team."

Monica added the names, then looked at Gran. "So you think it was one of the kids?"

She shrugged. "I've no idea, love, but I figure they are the best people to ask about Emily's movements. Now"—she eased up out of the armchair and straightened her clothes—"if you'll excuse me, I have a burlesque class to get to."

CHAPTER
FOUR

Jordan left along with Gran. Monica, Jenna, and I had just decided we'd head to Brewed Awakening, the bar where Monica worked, for a nightcap before heading home, when shouts of "Fire! Fire!" came from outside. Barreling out of The Dusty Attic we stood on the sidewalk, craning our necks to see what all the excitement was about.

"Look!" Jenna pointed. The sun had almost set while we'd been inside and now, in the twilight, we could see the faint flicker of flames coming from the beach. She ran, calling out over her shoulder, "Come on!"

I followed, but Monica hung back. "You guys go ahead. Us vamps are about as keen on fire as we are on sunlight. I'll meet you at the bar later, okay?"

I stopped and turned to face my friend. "You're sure?"

She nodded. "Absolutely. Go check it out and you can tell me all about it later."

I ran after Jenna, out of breath by the time I got to the parking lot in front of the beach. A fire truck was there, lights flashing, hosing down one of the beach huts. Jenna was taking photos on her phone.

"Do you know whose hut it is?" I asked, puffing and nursing a stitch in my side.

"Nope." she said, eyes intent as she watched the firemen do their job. A patrol car pulled up and Officer Miles climbed out, eyes sweeping over the crowd that had gathered before coming to rest on me.

"Should have known," she snapped, stalking past me, back ramrod straight. Jenna looked at me and I shrugged. Liliana had never liked me, and since breaking up with Jackson her dislike had only grown.

"We meet again." I jumped when Jackson's breath blew hot in my ear.

Hand to my chest I spun. "Geez. Don't do that!" I wheezed, heart pounding from the fright he'd given me.

He grinned. "Sorry bout that." He wasn't sorry at all, I could tell by the twinkle in his eyes.

"Why are you here?" I demanded, "Since when do fires require a detective?"

"Since the beach hut in question was torched on

purpose." Jackson slid his hands into the pockets of his jeans and rocked back and forth on his heels, his eyes not missing a thing as he watched the firemen clean up. It hadn't taken them long to douse the flames, and from where I was standing, the beach hut hadn't sustained too much damage. They'd gotten here fast.

"Arson?" Jenna asked, switching her phone to record mode and swinging it in Jackson's direction.

"No comment," was his dry response. Jenna sniffed and turned her phone off.

"Off the record," she said.

"Sure," Jackson agreed. "Possible arson. Preliminary report from the fire chief says it looks like they used an accelerant on the outside of the hut, rear corner."

"This would make the third suspicious fire this month," Jenna said, more to herself than us, and I could practically see the cogs turning in her head. She was already outlining a potential story.

"There have been other fires?" I hadn't seen nor heard any evidence that Whitefall Cove had a firebug, but Jackson was nodding his head.

"A brush fence was set on fire last week, on Rigby Road, and the week before that a trash can on Peter Street."

"So the arsonist is escalating." They'd progressed from small items, to a building structure. Granted, it wasn't a huge one, and the chances of someone being hurt were minimal, but still, someone had set these fires intentionally.

"Probably kids," Jackson said. "Bored over summer vacation. We see a spike in this sort of thing every year."

Something caught his attention over my shoulder. His eyes narrowed and his hands slid free from his pockets. "Ah!" he said. "Just the person I was looking for. Excuse me, ladies." And with that he was gone.

I watched with interest as he hurried over to a man I vaguely recognized, dressed in a sharp navy pinstripe suit, a blue tie pulled loose at the collar. I put him to be late thirties, early forties.

"Detective." The man nodded, looking from Jackson to the beach hut and back again. "What are you thinking? Vandals? Or the arsonist?" I blinked in surprise. So the man knew that we potentially had a fire starter in our midst. Jenna was busy snapping photos of the two men talking.

"Daniel Griffin"—she nodded toward the man—"is gunning for the Mayor's job this election."

"Griffin? As in Jacob's dad?"

"Uncle. Long-standing town council member."

"Is Mayor Burch retiring?" This was the first I'd heard of it, but then I'd been living in East Dondure for the last five years and local politics held little interest for me. I guess now that I was a local business owner, I'd better start paying attention.

"Elaine? Not that I know of. She's only sixty, and a young sixty at that." Jenna scoffed, as if the very idea was ludicrous. "She plays tennis and golf every week, plus handles a full workload with the town council. No, I can't see her retiring anytime soon. Not voluntarily anyway. This is the first time in years that anyone has run against her as mayor."

I opened my mouth to ask her why she thought Daniel Griffin, mayoral candidate, was at the scene of an arsonist attack, when she shushed me. "Sssh. I'm trying to listen. I think the beach hut might be his."

Clamping my lips shut, I did as instructed, listening in to their conversation.

"When was the last time you were here?" Jackson asked.

Daniel shrugged. "I haven't been down to the beach all summer, I've been busy with planning an election campaign, no time for anything else."

"And does anyone else have access?"

"I'm not sure. I guess?" With his hands on his hips and legs braced apart he glared at Jackson. "I thought you said the fire was lit on the outside? What does it matter who has access?"

Jackson's eyebrows shot up. "Sounding a little defensive there, Councilman."

Daniel relaxed his stance and ran a weary hand around the back of his neck. "You're right. I'm sorry. God, it's just this is the last thing I need to be dealing with right now, you know? I keep the key to the cabin in my home office. Family members are welcome to use it, but I haven't had any of them approach me this summer, so no, I don't think anyone has been in there for a while."

"And you're insured?"

"It's just a beach hut, but yes, I'm insured. Insurance covered a new paint job a couple of years ago when vandals graffitied it."

Ah, that would explain the vibrant blue paint when the other huts didn't look quite as fresh.

"A second claim in as many years will put my premium up," Daniel grumbled.

"Do you know anyone who would want to target you?" Jackson asked and Daniel laughed.

"Are you serious? I'm running for mayor! Of course I have enemies. But why attack my beach hut of all things? That's not exactly going to hurt me, inconvenience me, yes, but it will not jeopardize my campaign."

"Have you received any threats?" Jackson pressed.

Daniel shook his head. "No, nothing like that. I run a clean ship and I'll win the election fair and square."

"Okay, I think that's it for now. If you hear anything, remember anything, call me." Jackson shook his hand and the two men parted ways.

Jenna turned to me, chewing on her lip.

"What?" I asked.

"I'm not sure. It's a stretch and there probably isn't a connection, but Jacob's girlfriend is killed on the beach, then Jacob's uncle's beach hut is torched."

"So you're saying it's not a coincidence?"

She sucked her lips in and then released them with a pop. "Undecided. If an arsonist were to turn killer, he'd most likely burn his victims."

"What if the killer came back to destroy evidence?" I clasped her arm. "What if the killer is using the recent arson attacks to his advantage?"

"So you think there is something in the beach hut? And that's why the killer tried to destroy it?"

"It's a lead!" I finally felt I had something to follow, a thread to tug on to unravel the mystery of Emily's death. "We just need to wait for this lot to clear out so we can take a look."

As if sensing what we were plotting, Liliana strode past, knocking my shoulder as she went. I staggered back, rubbing my arm. She didn't pause, didn't look back, didn't apologize.

"Oh, geez," Jenna whispered, slinging an arm around my shoulders. "We'd better stay out of her way until the frost is over."

"The frost will never be over with that one," I muttered, watching Liliana through narrowed eyes as she opened the door of her patrol car. Jackson approached her, face angry, and Jenna and I watched unabashedly as the two of them argued, right in front of us.

"I feel like we shouldn't be watching this," Jenna whispered. "But I also feel like we should pull up a chair and bring out the popcorn."

"I'm right there with you." We couldn't hear what they were saying, but the facial expressions and arm gestures revealed a very heated discussion was going down. And then the pair of them looked my way. Ducking my chin I turned my back to them and pretended to be busy with my phone.

"Oh!" Jenna snorted. "Shoulda guessed."

"Don't," I warned

"What? I get it now. She thinks you're the reason they broke up."

"Well, I'm not." I knew I was pouting. And I knew that because I had originally thought that too. That Jackson had broken up with her because he had feelings for me. He'd blown up my phone while I'd been in Australia. And ever since I'd been waiting for him to ask me out, only nothing. Zip. Nada.

It reminded me a little too much of Blake and the way he'd bailed, leaving me hanging with no idea what had happened.

"And now you're frowning." Jenna pressed a thumb hard between my eyebrows.

"Hey!" I protested, rubbing at the spot.

CHAPTER
FIVE

Half an hour later we returned, creeping along the row of beach huts like fugitives. I was paranoid Liliana was lying in wait and I wouldn't put it past her to slap me in cuffs and take me down to the station for interfering with a crime scene.

Archie appeared out of nowhere, scaring the ever-living-beejeesus out of me.

"Archie!" I whispered, crouching to give him a pat. "What are you doing here? I thought Gran was dropping you home?"

Meow.

"Maybe you left a window open, and he got out?" Jenna said, dropping to her knees in the sand to give Archie a fuss.

"Probably. He likes the beach." Standing back up, I

looked at the huts in the darkness. The once bright blue hut belonging to Daniel Griffin was now smeared with soot, and the scent of smoke and water hung heavy in the air.

"I'm going to look around." Approaching the hut, I peered around the corner, but didn't have a direct line of sight to the parking lot. Well, that was something. If I couldn't see the lot, then Liliana couldn't see me. If she was still there.

In between the narrow space between two huts, the structures blocked almost all light. Dark and spooky didn't begin to cover it. Pulling out my phone, I turned on the flashlight app and swung it around. Nothing. Moving back to the front of the hut, I tried the door. Locked.

"You aren't thinking of breaking in, are you?" Jenna asked.

"Nope." I wasn't that stupid. Liliana was just dying for an excuse to arrest me; I wasn't about to make it easy for her.

"The damage isn't that bad." Jenna was shining the light from her phone on the rear of the hut and I moved to join her. "Just superficial. But look at this." She nudged a pile of debris with her foot. "It looks like someone set fire to something else and the fire caught hold of the hut."

"By accident?"

"Hard to say."

Archie's meowing interrupted us. Long, loud, and insistent, followed by a girl's voice saying, "Go away, go away!"

"Archie?" I followed the sounds into the shrubs behind the huts only to discover him winding around and head butting the crouched figure of Hannah Burton.

"Hannah? What are you doing back here?"

Knowing she'd been busted she stood, dusting off her legs. "Stupid cat," she muttered to Archie, who was now nosing at a backpack I hadn't seen earlier. She reached for it, but I darted forward and snatched it from her grasp.

"Hey!" she protested, making another grab for the bag, but I held it out of reach. "Give that back! It's mine!"

"What do you have in here that you don't want me to see?"

"Nothing!" But the look of guilt gave her away. Keeping one eye on her, I unzipped the backpack and peered inside. Not much to see. Some books, a scarf. But Hannah's agitation told me there was more to this.

"Jenna!" I called. "Come here a second. I need your light."

"What's up?" Jenna appeared seconds later. "Oh, Hi Hannah, what are you doing here?"

"That's what I asked. She was crouched in the bushes. Hiding."

51

Jenna pinned Hannah with a look. "Oh."

"Exactly. I was just going to take a peek in her bag, but I could use your light."

"No problem. Here." Jenna shone the light from her phone into Hannah's backpack and that's when I saw it. A lighter. Up ending the bag, I dumped all the contents onto the ground. The scarf unraveled, revealing a can of lighter fluid.

"Oh, Hannah." Jenna sighed, shaking her head.

Tears rolled down Hannah's cheeks, but she didn't say a word. Jenna and I looked at each other.

"Did you light the fire?" I asked. She nodded.

"Why?" I pressed. She shrugged.

"Did you light the other fires?" Jenna asked. "The fence and the bin?"

Hannah nodded, shoulders hunched forward. She sniffed, wiped her nose on the back of her hand.

"Were you trying to set fire to the hut?" I nodded towards the Griffins' beach hut.

"No! That was an accident. I just..." She broke off, sniffed again, looked up at the night sky and let out a shuddering sigh. "I couldn't leave it unfinished. I don't know why, honestly. But I had to come back and finish it."

"Finish what?"

"What I started."

"What did you start Hannah?"

She looked around, eyes a little wild. Dropping the

backpack, I stepped over the contents and grasped her hands. "Take a deep breath and tell me exactly what happened."

She did. "I was here last night," she said, "to set the fire."

"Only something stopped you. Emily. Was she here last night?"

Hannah nodded. "Yes." She sniffed again and Jenna handed her a tissue.

"What happened?"

"I didn't mean to kill her! I swear!" Hannah wailed, face distraught. Jenna and I stiffened but listened as Hannah spoke, her words running together, "She texted me, asked me to meet her here. She was upset. Like, *really* upset. Only I got here before her and while I was waiting the idea to light a fire just came to me. So I dragged all these dead leaves and driftwood and stuff and was getting ready when Emily arrived, and she knew, before I even lit it, that I was the one lighting fires and I panicked."

The tears were falling thick and fast and she drew in a shuddering breath.

"Then what happened?" I pressed.

"I pushed her," Hannah whispered, "and she fell. And the sound of her head hitting a rock... it was awful. She just lay there, not moving, and I knew I'd killed her." Another pause, then she whispered, "I ran away."

Jenna and I looked at each other over Hannah's bent head.

"Was that the last time you saw her?" Jenna asked.

Hannah nodded. "I should have told someone. Should have got help. But I was too scared." So Hannah had left her friend unconscious on the beach. Not much of a friend.

"But you came back. Tonight. To light the fire. Why?"

"I had to! I can't explain it. All last night I resisted, I wanted to come back and light it, but Emily was here and I couldn't face what I'd done. But then this morning... you found her. So I knew I could come back tonight and light the fire."

Hannah was a pyromaniac. She couldn't resist the compulsion to light fires. And her version of events, of pushing Emily and Emily hitting her head fitted with the blunt trauma injury they'd found.

"Keep an eye on her," I said to Jenna, moving away. "I'm calling Jackson."

"Sure."

Leaving them in the bushes, I made my way back to the beach and the hut, dialing Jackson as I went.

"Are you okay?" Jackson answered.

"You know it is entirely possible for people to answer the phone with a greeting and not a question," I responded.

"I saw the way Liliana treated you tonight," he

ground out, clearly still angry at his ex. "I'm sorry she did that."

"It's okay Jackson. She's hurting. I get that."

I dug through the sand at the back of the hut with one hand, feeling around until I found it. The rock, hidden beneath a layer of sand, the one that Emily cracked her head on.

"What are you doing?" Jackson asked. "You're making strange grunting noises."

"I know who's been lighting the fires. And how Emily got the injury to the back of her head."

"Oh?"

"Meet me at the Griffins' beach hut." I hung up, took some snaps of the bloodstained rock I'd just unearthed, then made my way back to where Jenna and Hannah were waiting.

"Detective Ward is on his way," I said. Hannah nodded.

Scooping up her empty backpack, I handed it to her. "Gather up your stuff." While she did that, I whispered to Jenna that I'd found the rock and she hightailed it back to the hut to take her own photos.

"Come on, Archie." I picked up my cat, promising an extra special treat for revealing Hannah's hiding spot to us. Without him we'd have never known she was there.

It didn't take Jackson long to reach us. Hannah and I had joined Jenna at the rear of the hut.

"Would someone like to tell me what's going on?" he asked, doing his best to shake sand out of his shoe.

I filled him in on what Hannah had told us. He studied the frightened teenager before him, shaking his head.

"Were you hiding in the bushes this entire time?" Jackson asked her.

She nodded.

"Why? Were you going to light another fire? Did you decide that the beach huts made perfect targets?"

"No." She sniffed. "I just... it was where Emily... I couldn't...."

I sympathized. She thought her friend had died here and couldn't bring herself to leave, couldn't forgive herself for what she'd done, and for running away rather than fetching help.

"What happens now?" I asked, already knowing the answer. Jackson had no other choice than to arrest Hannah.

Jackson pressed his lips into a grim line. "I'm going to take Hannah to the station where she'll be questioned about her involvement in Emily's death – and charged with arson. I can't rule out a manslaughter charge at this point." He swung his head toward Jenna. "This has to stay off the record. I'd ask you to delete your photos, but I'm pretty sure you have them backed up to the cloud already."

She gave him a cheeky grin but didn't reply. Jenna

wasn't a cutthroat journalist. She knew Hannah's arrest would have an impact on the town, and Hannah's family. She'd handle the story with sensitivity.

"I'm going to send Officer Miles back to re-evaluate the scene," he added, cocking his head toward the rock we'd unearthed.

"Right," I said. "Well if you don't need me, Archie and I will head home." I had no desire to bump into Liliana again. She'd no doubt be furious we'd discovered something she'd missed, but to be fair, the rock was submerged beneath layers of sand. We'd only found it because we'd been looking for it.

"I will need your version of tonight's events," Jackson said, taking Hannah's arm and leading her around the front of the huts and towards the parking lot. "But it can wait until tomorrow. Call into the station when you have the time."

"Will do."

Jenna and I stood side by side, watching until they were out of sight. As soon as I heard the roar of Jackson's engine I turned to her.

"Right, we probably have about five minutes, maybe less, until Officer Miles turns up."

Jenna frowned at me. "Okay?"

I rolled my eyes, dropping Archie to the sand and hurrying back to the space between the huts. "To see if we can find Emily's bag or phone!"

"Oh! Right!" Jenna hurried after me, dropping to her knees by my side as I dug my hands through the sand, searching. "It would make sense if she fell here, was knocked out, that maybe her phone is here too. I doubt her bag would be buried beneath the sand though, way too big not to be noticed."

"True." I fanned my fingers out beneath the sand and frantically crawled along. Nothing. And time was running out.

"I don't think it's here," Jenna said, sitting back on her haunches and dusting off her hands.

"Wait. Lemme see if Gran has her number. If she calls it, maybe we'll hear it ring."

I called Gran who answered the phone breathless.

"Gran? Are you okay?"

A pause. "I'm fine, Harper love. What is it?" She sounded... different. Odd. Her voice lower than usual.

"I was wondering if you had Emily's number? And if you do, can you call it? I want to see if I can hear it ring. Maybe she dropped it at the beach and it's covered in sand."

"Why didn't the cops think of this?" she asked.

"They probably did. They can trace a phone these days so I'd imagine it's probably turned off, or the battery is dead. This is a long shot."

"Or it's at the bottom of the ocean," Jenna cut in.

"Or that." I agreed. But Emily's murder had been one of opportunity. It wasn't premeditated. How would the killer know that she'd be knocked out in her scuffle with Hannah? I'm sure that's what happened. The blow hadn't killed her, merely rendered her unconscious. Someone else had been on the scene and they may have taken her phone and bag to dump with the body. All I could do was hope they'd missed something.

"Okay Gran, I'm hanging up. Call Emily's cell, and if it goes to voicemail, don't leave a message, just hang up. If the phone's here, I'm hoping we'll hear it ring."

"On it." Gran hung up.

Jenna and I looked at each other. We didn't have much time until Liliana arrived.

"We'll give it—" I started to say, only to suddenly stop when I heard a phone ringing.

"Oh my God!" Jenna grabbed my arm so hard I'd have bruises. We looked at the structure before us. "It's coming from *inside the hut*!"

CHAPTER

SIX

Chewing on my nail, I pondered what to do. Liliana would be here any minute and she wouldn't be happy to see me, but this was a major breakthrough.

"You go," I said to Jenna. "No point you being in the line of fire too."

"You're sure?" Jenna hesitated.

"Absolutely. Go meet Monica, let her know what's happened. After I'm done here, I'm going to check in on Gran. I think something's up." She'd sounded strange on the phone and given she was eighty and lived alone... I tried not to dwell on the possibilities.

I walked with Jenna to the parking lot and watched as she hurried towards the main street, no doubt taking a detour to the *Whitefall Cove Tribune* offices on the way. Crossing my arms, I waited for the patrol car I knew was on the way. I didn't have to wait long. Headlights swung into the parking lot, blinding me with their intensity before flicking off.

"Why are you here, Jones?" Liliana popped the trunk and climbed out of the patrol car, her blue uniform still crisp although she'd been wearing it all day. I wondered if it was a fae thing that had her looking cool and calm no matter the weather?

"I made another discovery." I did my best not to appear on the defensive, made a conscious effort not to cross my arms across my chest, no matter how much I wanted to.

"*Another* discovery?" Her eyes bored into me, cold as steel.

"I was the one who found Hannah hiding in the bushes. And the rock we think Emily hit her head on."

She paused in lifting a case out of the trunk, muttered something under her breath I didn't catch, then continued on, slamming the trunk.

"And what's that?" She stepped onto the sand, heading toward the beach huts.

"Emily's phone is in the Griffins' beach hut."

She scoffed at that, not even pausing. I hurried after her.

"Doubtful. We have IT tracing it."

"Have you tried calling her number?" I asked. "Because Gran just did and coincidentally a phone rang at the exact same time from inside the hut."

We reached the blue hut in question and Liliana put the case on the sand, flicking the locks to reveal forensic paraphernalia.

"Thanks for the information. I'll check it out." She hoisted out a lantern, flicked it on, the light illuminating the dark alley between the two huts. "You can go." She paused. "Jesus. What were you doing here, building sandcastles?" This time giving me a look that told me she was less than impressed.

I shrugged my shoulders. "We were looking for her phone. Figured if the rock was hidden beneath the sand then maybe Emily dropped her phone and it got buried too."

Liliana paused, considering what I'd said.

"Look, Liliana," I began, wanting to clear the air with her, "I know you don't like me—"

"It's Officer Miles." She cut me off. "And I am not having this conversation with you. I'm here to do a job. I suggest you let me do it or I'll arrest you for obstruction."

Okay then. "Right. Well, I'll be off then." I hurried away. It wasn't until I was halfway up the street and heading toward The Dusty Attic to collect my car I realized I'd lost track of Archie.

"Damn it." Swiveling on my heel, I headed back toward the beach. Loath to call Archie's name and alert Liliana to the fact I was still around, I peered into the darkness, hoping to glimpse orange fur. And that's when I heard it. A sniffling sound. Confused, I silently made my way onto the sand and toward the huts where Liliana was working. I kept to the shadows, my stomach clenched in case she spotted me and arrested me. I wouldn't put it past her.

It wasn't until I was almost upon her that I realized what I'd heard was the sound of someone crying. Liliana was softly sobbing. I clapped a hand over my mouth and backed away. She would kill me if she knew I'd heard her, witnessed her moment of weakness. Was she crying because of me? Surely not! Maybe she'd known Emily and having to investigate her murder was salt in the wound?

Archie leaped out, playfully tackling my ankle, and it was all I could do not to scream. Scooping him up, I hurried away, trying to be as quiet as possible while I practically sprinted from the beach. I didn't slow until I reached the parking lot at the rear of my bookstore. Digging out my keys, I unlocked my car and deposited Archie on the passenger seat before sliding behind the wheel.

"It's getting late, huh, boy?" I said, snapping my seatbelt into place and reversing. "We'll swing by Gran's house first, then home."

The lights were out at Gran's and at first I thought she must have gone out. Gran never had a shortage of dates and her social life was more active than mine. I sat in the car out front of her cottage, engine idling, debating whether or not to leave her a note, when Archie scratched at the car door.

"What's wrong?" He stood on his rear legs, front paws at the window, and looked over his shoulder at me, his eyes beseeching.

"You want to see Gran?" I asked him, ruffling his fur. "I don't think she's home, but okay. I guess we can check. I'll leave her a note that we dropped in for a visit."

Killing the engine, I opened the door and Archie launched across my lap before I could move. I laughed at his enthusiasm and locked up the car, following him to the front door. I knocked, not expecting an answer.

"Help." Faint. Feeble. From inside the house.

"Gran?" Panic rose in me. Had that been Gran's voice calling for help? With a snap of my fingers I unlocked the front door and hurried inside, Archie streaking ahead of me.

"Where are you?" Flicking lights on as I went, I stuck my head into each room.

"Kitchen."

I sprinted down the hallway and skidded into the kitchen to find Gran sprawled on the kitchen floor, her face contorted in agony. Quickly rushing to her side, I took one of her hands in both of mine.

"What happened?"

"Threw my back out." She gasped. "It's been

twinging all day and silly me ignored it. Tsk, stupid old body."

"Why didn't you tell me when I called? How long have you been like this?" Now I knew why she'd sounded strange on the phone. She'd been in pain.

"Can't reach the phone. Or my wand. Happened shortly after you called. I tried Emily's number like you wanted and I turned to put the kettle on for a nice cup of tea when *snap*. Dropped me like a sack of potatoes."

"Here. This will hold you until I get a healer here." I held my hands over her body and pushed my magic into her, numbing her pain. Her face immediately relaxed, and she moved as if to get up.

"Uh uh." I placed a hand on her shoulder and held her to the floor. "Don't move. You're not fixed; I've just eased your pain. Is Agnes still your healer?" Agnes was a member of our coven, the Sisters of the Sacred Flame.

"Yes." Archie curled up by Gran's side, purring. Idly she stroked him. Good. He could keep her calm and distracted while we waited for Agnes. Pulling out my phone, I called her and she promised she'd be right over.

"How long have you had a bad back?" I asked Gran, sitting cross-legged by her side while we waited.

"A long time, love. It's just wear and tear, a body getting old, that's all."

"Well, maybe it's time to slow down, just a tad?"

"Hah!" She snorted. "I'll slow down when I'm pushing up daisies."

I laughed, but on the inside I worried. Gran wasn't getting any younger, she'd be eighty-one soon, and I didn't want to think about life without her.

"Don't you be getting maudlin on me, child," she warned, knowing where my thoughts were heading.

I forced a smile. "I wouldn't dream of it."

"YoooHooo!" A voice came from the front of the house where I'd left the door open.

"Back here, Agnes!" I climbed to my feet and greeted Agnes as she bustled into the kitchen.

"Your back again, Alice?" she asked sympathetically, dropping a medicine bag on the kitchen table and digging around in it. "Boil the kettle, will you, Harper love?"

I did as instructed, watching as Agnes, a spritely seventy-two-year-old, ground up herbs using the mortar and pestle she'd brought with her. Once that was done she passed her wand over Gran's body, running it from head to toe three times while chanting a healing spell.

"Okay, you can help her up." Agnes stood back with a satisfied nod and I stepped forward to pull Gran to her feet, keeping a firm hold in case she felt dizzy.

"Thanks Agnes." Gran grinned. "You're a doll."

"Drink the herbs Alice," Agnes ordered. "And then we'll have that whisky you've been promising me."

I rolled my eyes. I knew where this was leading. Leaving both witches at the kitchen table, I finished making the herbal tea for Gran, sending it floating across the room with a wave of my magic. While she sipped at the brew, I lifted three glasses from the overhead cupboard and sent them to the table too, before following with the bottle of whisky Gran kept in the pantry.

"You missed your last appointment, Alice." Agnes was lecturing Gran, and I bit back a smile at the contrite look on Gran's face. "You know you need regular treatments if you don't want to experience more episodes like this."

I paused in pouring out a shot of whisky. "So this happens frequently?"

Agnes tapped the glass to bring my attention back to pouring. "It won't happen at all if she keeps up her treatment." There was a distinct twang of sarcasm in Agnes tone. Gran gulped down the rest of her tea and the cup settled onto the saucer with a clatter.

"Tastes just like the swill Harper serves up at the bookstore."

I smirked. "Oh good. You're feeling better."

Handing her a whisky, I clinked glasses with them both before gulping down the golden liquid, blinking as it burned a path down my throat before pooling in my stomach, the heat radiating out and warming me from head to toe. Not necessarily a good thing on a hot summer night. Sweat beaded my brow, and I fanned myself.

"Young-un can't handle her liquor." Agnes reached for the bottle and poured herself another shot. "Alice?"

Gran held her glass out and Agnes dutifully poured. She eyeballed me, but I shook my head. I knew better than to try to keep pace with these two. I'd seen Gran in action before. She could drink anyone I knew under the table and turn up the following morning as fresh as a daisy. I wasn't falling for it. Not again.

Leaning over, I dropped a kiss on Gran's cheek. "You two behave, okay? And, Gran? Please look after yourself. You scared me." My voice cracked and emotion threatened to consume me.

"I'm fine, sweetheart." Gran patted my hand. "And as much as it pains me to admit, Agnes is right. I just need to make sure I see her every month so she can top up her healing spell and I'll be fine. I was so caught up training the kids for the talent competition I totally forgot about it."

Smiling tightly, I bid them both goodnight. It had been a long day, and I badly needed to decompress.

CHAPTER
SEVEN

It was almost ten o'clock when a knock at the front door roused me from my semi-catatonic state on the sofa. Archie was snoozing at my feet and the television was blaring, but I couldn't say what the program was. I'd put it on for background noise more than anything. Gran's fall worried me. I couldn't stop thinking about her lying on the floor in the dark, unable to move. Maybe I shouldn't have moved out.

Flinging open the door, I blinked in surprise to find Jackson, one arm leaning against the doorjamb, the other on his hip. His five o'clock shadow was more pronounced, giving him an edgy, almost dangerous look.

"Can I come in?" He straightened, his eyes traveling over me from head to toe. Goosebumps danced across my skin and my breath hitched in my throat. There was something different about him tonight. Something... primal. I felt it coming off him in waves and my inner witch sighed in delight.

"Sure." Turning away, I left the door open and headed back to the sanctuary of the sofa where a bottle of red wine, already opened, waited. "Glasses are in the kitchen," I said, refilling my glass. I heard him opening cupboard doors until he found what he was looking for. Helping himself to the wine, he settled in an armchair and took a sip.

"It's good."

"I know." God, such banal conversation. Why was he here? Drinking wine in my living room. Not that I was complaining, I always had enjoyed having him around, but my recent record with men and relationships wasn't good and I no longer trusted my own judgement. The way Jackson had looked at me when I opened the door was not the way a man looked at a woman he considered just a friend. Another shiver danced over my skin.

"I thought I was doing the right thing," he suddenly blurted out, swirling the wine in his glass, his eyes tracking the liquid as if fascinated by it, "but at every turn I was just hurting someone. Her. You." He sighed. "I think I knew from the very first moment I set eyes on you that we could have something... special. That there was a connection between us."

I froze in place, not daring to believe what I was hearing. Biting my tongue, I waited for more. He delivered.

"But I'm a decent man. An honorable man. I thought the feelings I had for you were a passing fancy. I liked Liliana. A lot. And the last thing I ever wanted to do was hurt her. But when you were in Australia, with him? It tortured me." He looked up and our eyes met. I could see the pain reflected in the green depths and my heart hurt. I'd had no idea. I thought the crush I had on him was one hundred percent one sided.

"And that's when I knew unequivocally that it would never work with Liliana. That it wasn't fair to her."

"So you broke up with her."

He heaved a big sigh. "She took it incredibly badly. She knew it was because of you." Before I could protest his eyes snapped back to me. "Oh, I never told her how I felt about you. Just how I didn't feel about her. But she knew. She'd sensed it from the beginning, I think."

I suspected he was right. Flashes of them together, of her staking her claim on him with a hand on his arm and a glare at me. She'd suspected something wasn't right in her relationship, all right. A woman sensed these things.

He laughed, a desperate, anguished, laugh. "And

then you came back from Australia, without him." He swallowed, eyes beseeching. "You and he... did you?"

I cocked my head. He wasn't asking what I thought he was asking. Was he? But the way his fingers were clenching the stem of the wineglass, so tight it would surely break, and the almost desperate pleading in his eyes.

"Nothing happened with Blake." I wasn't one to kiss and tell, but I also wasn't one to prolong someone's pain, and I could see that the very thought of me and Blake together was torturing Jackson. "We shared a kiss or two, nothing more."

Silence settled over us, thick and heavy, yet the relief on his face was unmistakable. He relaxed into the chair, the grip on the wine glass easing. When he spoke next, it was to continue with the telling of his relationship with Liliana. "I was a free man, but I couldn't tell you how I felt because she was so hurt. I couldn't do it to her, I couldn't rub her face in it. So I waited."

My heart stopped in my chest.

"But now I'm done waiting." He stood, placed his wineglass on the coffee table and in one long stride was in front of me, hands tugging me to my feet. My mouth dropped open, but I had no words. I vaguely wondered if I was dreaming, if the whisky I'd had at Gran's house, combined with the red wine, had addled my brain and conjured him up from my imagination, for surely this was a dream come true.

"Harper," he whispered it against my lips, and it was the most erotic thing I'd ever experienced. One big hand wrapped around my nape, the other slid to the small of my back where he tugged me against him, our bodies flush. My heart went into overdrive, the blood rushing through my body at an alarming speed, heat and fire sizzling my nerve endings everywhere we touched. Wrapping my arms around his neck, I pressed against him.

It was entirely possible fireworks went off. Or maybe it was just static electricity, but the zap that shot through me when our lips finally touched set off an avalanche of feelings. Want. Need. Lust. With a sweep of his tongue he demanded entry, and I gave it, lost in the touch of him, the taste of him. He was like nectar I couldn't get enough of, each taste more addictive, more demanding.

The kiss went on forever and ended all too soon. The jarring sound of his phone had him tearing his mouth away with a curse and I smiled, a satisfied, purely feminine smile.

"You could ignore it," I purred, running my hands through his hair, luxuriating in the thick strands sliding through my fingers.

"I could." He growled, dropping his mouth to my neck, the scrape of his stubble intoxicating. "But I won't." Dragging himself out of my arms, he crossed to the other side of the room, putting distance between us, before barking into his phone. "What?"

I watched, dazed and heated with passion as Jackson listened to whoever was on the other end of the line, all the time, his eyes hot and dark, were on me. I swallowed. He looked like he wanted to eat me alive, and heaven help me, I was all for it.

He ended the call, and I knew what was coming. "You have to go."

He nodded. "I have to go. But before I do, there's just one thing."

"Oh?" Please let it be another kiss, but he stayed where he was, one corner of his mouth curling up in a smirk as if he knew exactly what I was thinking. "Will you go out with me?"

I blinked. Once. Twice. "As in... a date?"

"As in exactly like a date. Come with me to the talent competition."

"But what about Liliana?" I bit my lip, wanting nothing more than to go on a date with Jackson but mindful of the other woman's feelings.

"I broke up with her weeks ago. I'm done waiting. Liliana has been punishing me for something I didn't do, something that hadn't happened. I figure since she's all pissy about it anyway, I may as well do what I want and be damned."

He'd never looked hotter than he did in that

moment with blazing eyes and a flush across his cheekbones. "Stop looking at me like that," he growled, stalking close, dropping a rough kiss on my cheek before heading out the door. "I'm taking your silence as a yes. I'll pick you up at seven Saturday night."

"Okay," I squeaked, turning to look at the closed door with my hand over my thundering heart. I heard Jackson's car drive away, then turned to Archie, who cracked open one eye to look at me from his position on the end of the sofa. "What just happened?"

Meow? Scratching his ears, I sat back down and took a hefty gulp of wine. Just as I was reaching for my phone to text Jenna and tell her what had just transpired, it rang. Jenna's name flashed on the screen and I wondered if I was suddenly developing psychic abilities.

"I was just going to text you." I smiled, my excitement palpable.

"Oh? Well, I have news." Her voice was low, as if she didn't want to be overheard.

"Are you at work?" I couldn't hear any background noise, had expected her to be at Brewed Awakening with Monica, but from the lack of chatter and general rowdiness, I'd say not.

"I'm about to leave," she whispered, "but this couldn't wait."

I sobered. She sounded serious. Deadly serious.

"What is it?" My voice dropped, and I wondered why on earth I was whispering.

"Shit. Someone's coming." It sounded like she'd placed her hand over the phone, as if to muffle the sound. I waited, wondering what on earth was going on. I could hear shuffling and then she was back, whispering, "Someone's here."

"Wait, someone who shouldn't be there, you mean?"

"Yes."

The phone disconnected, and I immediately dialed Monica.

"Where *are* you guys?" Monica demanded, the background noise of the pub loud.

"I'm so sorry! I thought Jenna was with you. I asked her to tell you I couldn't make it—look, I'll explain everything, but.... can you get down to the *Tribune* offices? Jenna's there and someone is in the building. I think she needs help."

"On it." The dial tone buzzed in my ear. Clutching the phone to my chest, I sucked in a deep breath, trying to still my panic. Monica could get to Jenna faster than the cops. I just prayed she was fast enough. But who could have broken into the *Tribune*'s offices? And why? None of this was making any sense.

Half an hour later Jenna and Monica were in my living room finishing the rest of the wine and my heart rate had finally settled to a normal rhythm.

"So someone was definitely in the offices?"

Monica nodded. "I saw him. Dressed in black, wearing a balaclava."

"Was he there for Jenna, do you think?"

She shrugged. "Couldn't say for sure. He was heading toward the editor's office though, so I doubt it. I don't think he knew she was there, and I got her out so fast he would've been none the wiser."

"I called the cops, once we were outside, said that I thought I'd seen someone breaking in." Jenna was her usual cool, calm, and collected self, feathers one hundred percent unruffled.

"But she's a smart one." Monica tapped her temple, then pointed at Jenna. "She hid under a desk, just not her own."

"What?" I snorted. "Why?"

"Well, if he was after me, he'd come to my desk, right? And find me if I were hiding under it. So I figured, who is the least likely person on staff? Hatches, matches, and dispatches."

"I found her under the desk of the obituary reporter," Monica added at my puzzled look.

"Ahhh. Good thinking. So Jenna, what were you calling me about? Before you got interrupted by the intruder?"

Crossing one leg over the other, she leaned back in her armchair with a satisfied smirk on her face. "So getting back to the murder of Emily. She was going out with Jacob Griffin, correct?" I nodded, waving my hand for her to continue. "And she was knocked out—possibly abducted—from Jacob's uncle's beach hut."

"Well, outside of it, but go on." I nodded again.

"And the uncle, Daniel Griffin, is running for mayor."

I frowned. "You think this is political? What? Another candidate mistook Emily for Daniel?" That seemed too far-fetched, even for me, but Jenna was already shaking her head.

"Not at all. But I started looking into Daniel, more as a side story than anything else. And"—she cut me a sharp look—"this is why I was calling you. Daniel's campaign received a sizable donation from Richards, Jones, and Tennant." The law firm where Blake was a partner. My eyebrows shot into my hairline and Monica paused from opening another bottle of wine.

"Coincidence?" she purred in her sultry voice. "I think not. The plot thickens."

"Well, Blake was here to defend Gran," I pointed out. "He may have had other business meetings while he was in town."

Jenna shrugged, holding out her glass to Monica. "Perhaps. Anyway, that's what I was calling about. I don't know if it was Blake personally who made the donation. I'm still digging."

"Plus any information on Blake Tennant would be welcome. I don't get that guy." Monica sank back into her chair after topping up our glasses. "He swoops in, saves the day, gets the girl—only he doesn't, then disappears. What's up with that?"

"You know I'm not heartbroken over that, right?" I pointed out. "I liked Blake, sure, but..."

"But Jackson Ward." Jenna grinned, giving me a cheeky wink. I blushed. She pounced. "Something's happened. Spill."

"Oh my God, would you look at her face!" Monica crowed, "You're so right, Jenna. Come on, Harper, spill, what happened?" She tilted her face to the air and sniffed, narrowing her eyes. "He's been here. Recently. Tonight?"

I laughed, feeling the heat in my face. "Okay, okay, super sleuths, stand down. Yes, he was here."

"And?" they said in unison. Jenna shot Monica a look, which Monica returned.

"They kissed, didn't they?" Monica said to her.

"They so did." Jenna chuckled.

"Fine. We kissed. And yes, it was epic. And he's asked me out on a date." I couldn't contain the smile that curled my lips.

Throwing her hands up in the air in a dramatic gesture Monica raised her eyes to the ceiling. "Finally!"

"I'm so happy for you, Harper." Jenna laid a hand on my arm and squeezed.

"Thank you, guys. You know I love you like family."

"Ditto." We then launched into a lengthy discussion on what I should wear, until Monica suddenly froze, her vampire stillness rendering her a statue. It was eerie.

"What?" I asked, tossing a cushion at her to snap her out of it.

"I just remembered something." She blew out a breath, not because she needed oxygen, but to get her chest moving again. It was something vampires did to blend in, fake breathing. "Daniel Griffin bought a six-pack of beer the night before last."

"So?" No big surprise there. Lots of locals purchased take-away alcohol from Brewed Awakening.

"But he doesn't drink beer. We had quite the discussion over it recently. He's a scotch man. He doesn't like the flavor of beer. I even gave him several samples to try to win him over. Screwed up his face at each and every one."

"He could have been going to a function or event," Jenna said.

"No, but think about it. This case. The dead girl is a *teenager*. Her boyfriend is a *teenager*. Her boyfriend is also the nephew of Daniel Griffin."

I snapped my fingers. "You think Daniel bought the beer for Jacob."

"It's possible, I guess." Jenna nodded. "I'll talk to Daniel. I want an interview for the paper, anyway."

"He's not going to admit he purchased alcohol for his underage nephew," I pointed out.

"No, but he might just let it slip if he thinks it'll get his nephew off a murder charge."

CHAPTER
EIGHT

Jordan and I were unpacking a book order delivery the following morning when Jackson arrived. I straightened, putting a hand against my aching back, and waited.

"Oh, there he is, don't you look lovely today, Detective?" The ghost of Whitney Sims appeared as it did whenever Jackson and I were together in the store.

"Morning, Whitney." Jackson grinned, crossing to my side and dropping a kiss on my cheek. Jordan looked on in surprise. It was the first time she'd seen Whitney. Not to mention Jackson kissing me.

"Oh, my!" Whitney clasped her hands to her chest, looking from me to Jackson and back again. "Are you two an item now? How long have I been gone? Wait, you're not married are you?"

Jackson laughed. "No, we're not married."

Despite Whitney giving me the jitters, I leaned into Jackson's side, enjoying his warm strength. This was nice. "So, what brings you here?"

"Can't I just pop in to see you?" he teased.

"Yes, well, you know how I feel about that." I jerked my head toward Whitney who had drifted over to the boxes we were unpacking and was trying to lift a book out, only of course she couldn't. Because she was a ghost.

Jackson dropped his voice. "We could try an exorcism. Because I plan on dropping by a lot."

"As tempting as that is, I don't think I could do it to her," I whispered, watching as Whitney joyfully flitted through the bookshelves. "When she was alive she was a bully that no one liked, yet as a spirit... I've never seen her so happy. She's even happy to see Bruce!" Bruce was Whitney's husband, who'd been having an affair with Whitney's best friend—now my employee, Wendy—when Whitney was unfortunately murdered. In my store. Hence her haunting the place. But if Whitney could forgive her husband and best friend for their affair, who was I to deny her existence?

"Your call. I don't mind either way." Jackson helped himself to a coffee from the pot I kept on a dresser in the middle of the store, "Actually I dropped by to give you an update."

"Oh?"

"Wait!" Whitney drifted down from the

mezzanine. "What's happened? An update on what? Has there been another murder?"

"Emily Sherman." I nodded. "Did you know her?"

Whitney tapped her lip in thought. "Sherman, Sherman." She snapped her fingers. Well, mimicked snapping her fingers. Since she was incorporeal she made no sound. "Rose Sherman has property on Rigby Road." Whitney had been an office manager for a local construction company when she was alive, but had also been the town's realtor, and she knew every property in town. And its value.

"That's right. Rose was Emily's grandmother; Emily went to live with her when her parents died in a car accident."

Whitney nodded. "I remember that. Philip and Kelly. They had a little two-bedroom place on Damon Road."

"Yeah, well, big news, Rose was about to become a great-grandmother," Jackson muttered, keeping his voice low in case Jordan overheard.

"Emily was pregnant?" I hissed.

"That would explain the sudden growth explosion in the boob department," Gran murmured from beside me and I nearly shrieked at her sudden appearance.

"Gran! I didn't hear you come in."

"Evidently." Gran sniffed. "Whitney. How goes life in the spirit world?"

"Oh you know, can't complain."

"Gran, did you know about this? About Emily?"

She shrugged. "She'd either had a boob job or was knocked up. I hadn't decided which."

"Why didn't you say anything?"

"Because I wasn't sure. I figured if I waited a few more weeks, if she were preggers a belly would pop. If not, then definitely a boob job. But then I don't know where she'd get the money for that. I asked her if there was anything she wanted to talk about. Off the record type thing. She told me no. If there's one thing I know about teenagers, you can't push 'em."

"Fair point." I looked Gran up and down. Today she was dressed in grape leggings, a hot pink halter neck with a sequin heart covering the front, and bright red lipstick. "How are you feeling today? Should you be up and about?"

She waved away my concern. "Pft, stop fussing over me. I told you I'm fine. Agnes wove her magic as she always does and I'm fit as a fiddle once more."

"Did something happen?" Jackson was watching our exchange, his eyes narrowing. Dealing with Gran was a lot like dealing with a willful teenager. Difficult at times, but worth it in the end. "I'll tell you later."

To Gran I said, "So what brings you into the Dusty Attic this morning?"

"Actually, I came to see Jordan," Gran announced.

Jordan paused from where she'd continued to

unpack the books and, keeping a cautious eye on Whitney, glanced over.

"How would you like to join the winning team for the talent competition?" Gran's swagger was comical as she made her way toward Jordan, bedazzled flip-flops slapping on the floor.

"You're going ahead?" I'd thought with Emily's death that the team would have pulled out. Not to mention Hannah's arrest for arson.

"The others have trained so hard for this, it hardly seems fair to pull out now just because we're down a member."

"But..." Jordan scratched her head, brow furrowed. "Why me?"

Gran smacked her lips together and slung an arm around Jordan's shoulders. "I remember your audition, you were damn good."

"Not good enough to pick me for the team," Jordan shot back, shrugging Gran's arm off.

"Yes, well." Gran cleared her throat and tugged at the waistband of her leggings. "That's because you were pipped at the post by Hannah. I had you on my list, but the routine only called for three girls and three boys. You were always in my mind as a backup, but I couldn't tell you that and make you feel like second best poop now could I?"

I cringed at the wording but understood where Gran was coming from. She continued, "You've got talent. Raw talent, but with some coaching—from me —I'm confident I can get you up to speed."

"And I'd be partnered with Jacob?"

"Correct."

Jordan continued to stare at Gran, holding her gaze as she considered her options. To be honest, I was a little bit proud of my young employee. Gran had a way of roping people in with very little effort, but she was having to work for it with Jordan. This girl would not be a pushover. I crossed my arms and waited.

"I'd need a new dress."

"You're about the same size as Emily," Gran shot back.

Jordan shook her head. "No way I'm wearing a dead girl's dress."

"She didn't die in it."

"I don't care. What color is it?"

"It's blue."

"Deal breaker. I look like crap in blue. It has to be red."

Gran ground her teeth. "Fine. I'll get you a red dress."

"It can't be Emily's dress, spelled to look red. A new, different dress. And I have the right of refusal."

"You drive a hard bargain." Gran pouted.

"You need me." Jordan pounced. "And you know I don't like people in my personal space. I'm making a sacrifice for you if I do this. Least you can do is deliver on the dress."

"Deal."

"Pleasure doing business with you." Jordan held out her hand and Gran shook it, giving the young girl a wink.

Jackson leaned over. "I think that was the best thing I've ever seen."

I smiled. "It was, wasn't it?"

Jordan heard me and glanced over. She clapped her hand over her mouth. "I forgot about work! I'm sorry, Mrs. B, I can't. I promised Harper I'd help here."

"It's fine, Jordan, you go join the rehearsals. I can manage here just fine."

"Are you sure?" The excitement she'd managed to keep hidden during her negotiations with Gran burst through. She was practically bursting at the seams with it. I gave her a hug, although she didn't like people touching her. I'd seen the routine. She would be in physical contact with Jacob almost the entire time —best she got used to it. "Go. Have a good time. Do me proud."

"Thank you."

"Thanks, Harper." Gran reached up and pecked my cheek. "Drop on by later and see for yourself."

They left and suddenly it was just me and Jackson in the store. And Whitney. Thankfully ghost Whitney had a short attention span and was now cozied up in one of the bookshelves, reading. Well, her version of it.

"I'd better get going." Jackson drained his cup, setting it by the coffeepot.

"Thanks for dropping in with the update. So, do you know who the father is of Emily's baby?"

He shrugged. "We assume it's Jacob's. We'll have to get a sample of his DNA and get the lab to run tests to confirm though."

"It's so sad." I sighed. "Do you think that's why she was killed? Because she was pregnant and whoever the father is wasn't happy about it?"

"It's certainly motive," Jackson agreed, "but no more speculating until we get the results."

"One more question."

He snorted. "Just one, Jones?"

"For now. How far along was she?"

"Twelve weeks."

"It must have been getting difficult for her to hide it." I remembered what Gran had said about the increase in her boob size.

"Is that what she met Hannah for? To tell her about the baby?"

Jackson shrugged. "Hannah never found out why Emily wanted to meet. Emily busted her trying to light the fire and pegged that Hannah was the arsonist. They argued before Emily told her anything."

"What will happen with Hannah?"

WITCH WAY TO BEAUTY AND THE BEACH

"We have charged her with arson. It'll go before the court. Because she's a juvenile, she may get a good behavior bond along with some community service. And counseling. That's what I'll be pushing for."

His phone buzzed, and he glanced at the screen.

"Gotta go, work calls." He dropped a quick kiss on my lips, leaving them tingling, then headed out the door. "Bye, Whitney!"

"Oh! Bye, Jacks—" Poof. She was gone, and I was alone.

***

After a brief early morning rush, things had quieted down at The Dusty Attic. By lunchtime I'd unpacked and catalogued the book delivery, dusted and rearranged a few displays, and decided I'd close up and take Gran and the kids lunch.

The Silent Bite seemed a good choice. What teenager didn't like burgers and fries? Not to mention it was where Emily had an after-school job. The perfect opportunity to kill two birds with one stone. Locking the store, I slung my bag over my shoulder and headed up the street on foot.

Silent Bite had changed very little since I was a teenager. Black and white checkerboard tiles on the floor, red booths and counter, rock-and-roll paraphernalia on the walls. Joining the line, I studied the menu which hadn't changed either. The same burgers as when I'd been a teenager, the writing now faded.

After placing my order, I leaned forward and asked the lanky teenager working behind the counter, "Did you used to work with Emily?"

"What?" he squeaked, his voice at that awful stage, caught between a boy and a man.

"Emily. Did you work with her?" I repeated, holding my card and waiting for him to finish ringing me up so I could pay.

"Sure. Sometimes." He finished typing onto the screen—that was new—and I swiped my card.

"I heard she got fired. Know anything about that?" Putting my card back in my purse, I pulled out a bundle of notes. The teenager's eyes zeroed in on the cash. I wasn't above leaving him a generous tip in exchange for information. Seems he was a smart kid.

"She kept getting sick a lot. Like running off to puke halfway through her shift. The manager thought she was scoffing the food in between customers or something."

"Anything else?" I played with the cash. The teenager shrugged. "She was late a few times. I was here the day she got fired, and I overheard the manager telling her her standards had dropped."

"And what did Emily say to that?"

"She told him to drop dead."

"And what about her boyfriend, Jacob?"

"What about him?"

"Well, was everything okay between them? Had they been fighting?"

He shrugged. "I dunno. I don't keep tabs on her love life." He paused for a moment. "But she was different lately."

"Different how?"

"She was real happy for a while—which is saying something for Emily. Normally she treats us all like crap, but she was actually decent for a while. But then it changed."

"Changed?" I prompted.

"Moody. Different from before when she was just a bitch. And she puked and stuff. Wait? Was she sick? Did she have cancer? Was she having chemo? How come her hair wasn't falling out?"

"I don't think she had cancer." I shook my head. He cleared his throat and glanced over my shoulder. He had customers to serve, and I was holding up the line.

"One more question, I promise."

"Just one. I don't wanna get fired."

"Her happy mood? How long ago was that? Like in the last couple of months?"

He shook his head. "Nah, months ago. The last couple of months she's been weird. Weird for Emily, that is."

It tied in with her finding out she was pregnant.

"Thank you"—I glanced at his name badge—"Zack. You've been most helpful." I slid the notes across the counter to him and he palmed them before handing me my receipt.

"Your order shouldn't be too long, ma'am. If you'd like to wait over there."

I waited where he'd pointed, my mind going over what he'd told me. It was entirely possible that Jacob wasn't the baby's father, that Emily had been seeing someone before him. Had she known she was pregnant when she started dating Jacob? Only one way to find out. I'd go straight to the source and ask him.

NINE

This time when I stepped through the doors of the town hall I wasn't greeted with marshmallow goo. Instead Gran was taking the teenagers through a series of exercises, wands aloft as they hovered a foot from the floor. Seeing me, Gran waved them to relax, and they glided to the floor, touching down with a soft thud.

"Lunch!" I called, holding the bags of takeout up.

"Cool. I'm starved." Ethan reached me first and took a bag, digging inside and pulling out a burger. Ryan and Jacob were next, then Hannah, who approached somewhat sheepishly.

"Hannah." I greeted her with a nod.

"I'm so sorry for all the trouble I caused," Hannah said in a rush, twisting her hands together.

"Help yourself to a burger and we'll talk once

you've eaten, okay?" I hid my surprise that Hannah was even at rehearsals today. I'd thought for sure her parents would have grounded her.

"Hey, Harper." Jordan bounced up, a flush of color in her cheeks.

"Having fun?" I handed her a burger and a box of fries.

"This is so awesome."

"How's it going with Jacob?"

Jordan shrugged. "Yeah, fine."

"He hasn't been giving you a hard time that you've taken his girlfriend's place?" I pushed.

"What? No! He hasn't mentioned her. Not once." We both looked to where Jacob had joined his friends Ethan and Ryan. They were joking about as they ate. He hardly seemed heartbroken that his girlfriend was dead.

"Why don't you sit with Hannah?" I suggested to Jordan. "I think she could use a friend."

"Sure!" Jordan bounced off to sit next to Hannah who was looking pale and miserable. I still had three burgers in the bag. Mine, Gran's, and Sarah's. Sarah was in an animated conversation with Gran. They'd moved away and, despite not being able to hear what they were saying, the body language spoke volumes. Sarah was pissed and Gran wasn't having any of it.

Seeing me watching them, Sarah clamped her lips shut and flounced over to me, helping herself to a burger, and then stormed outside, the door slamming behind her.

"What's up with her?" Handing Gran her burger, I settled onto one of the wooden chairs set up around the perimeter of the hall. Gran sat next to me, unwrapping her burger.

"She's got her panties in a bunch because I paired Jordan with Jacob. She thinks she should be Jacob's partner and that Jordan can partner with Ethan."

"Ah." I nodded. "I heard that Sarah had eyes for Jacob."

"You'd have to be blind to miss it," Gran grumbled. "Girl has no shame, flirting outrageously."

"What does Jacob think? Does it make him uncomfortable?"

Gran narrowed her eyes at the three males across the room. "I think he thinks it's funny. He doesn't encourage her, not exactly, but he doesn't set her straight either. Which is why I think she thinks she has a shot."

We lapsed into silence while we ate our lunch. I'd forgotten drinks and gave Jordan my card to go buy milkshakes for everyone. Hannah went with her to help carry them back.

"How's Hannah doing?" I asked Gran, wiping my mouth with a napkin. "Do the others know she got charged with arson?"

Gran shrugged. "No one has said anything, so

probably not. Poor kid."

"Poor kid? Gran, she was deliberately setting fires. If we hadn't caught her, she could have ended up seriously hurting someone."

"That girl has been on her own for the last two years, practically bringing herself up. I'm not surprised something snapped."

"What do you mean? Adam and Jacqueline are still alive, still together. Aren't they?"

"They are," Gran said, "but since their boy died they've been in a spiral of grief and despair they still haven't surfaced from. Oh, they put food on the table, don't get me wrong, but that girl has been emotionally neglected."

"They had a son? Since when?" I knew nothing of this.

"Oh right. Happened while you were away. So Jacqueline falls unexpectedly pregnant at forty-eight. Can you imagine? They'd been trying for all those years to give Hannah a little brother or sister and had totally given up on it, when whammo, she gets knocked up."

"But she lost the baby?" I guessed.

Gran shook her head. "Nope. Carried to term, successful delivery. A little boy they named Adam Junior." Gran rolled her eyes at the name choice. "Then when he was four weeks old, he died."

"Oh, no!" How awful. I couldn't imagine. "How?

Why?"

"They say SIDS."

"Sudden Infant Death Syndrome. Oh, how awful. For everyone." Poor Hannah. She'd not only lost a little baby brother, she'd lost the emotional support of her parents when she'd needed it the most.

"Ever since, those folks have been going through the motions, but they're just shells."

I recalled that Adam worked as an accountant at The Bean Counter, and Jacqueline was a hairdresser at Curl Up & Dye. Gran nudged my arm, pulling me from my thoughts. "That lot look like they're up to something."

Jacob, Ethan, and Ryan had their heads together and were gathered around a backpack, looking very furtive indeed.

"I'll handle this." I headed across the room. The boys didn't hear me coming until I was upon them.

"What you got there, gentlemen?" I plucked the backpack from them. It was heavy, and I glanced at their startled faces before peering inside. Ah. Beer.

"Where did you get this?" I wasn't expecting an answer. I was pretty sure this was the beer that Daniel had purchased for his nephew.

"It's mine." Ethan made to grab for the bag, but I held it out of reach. There was a dynamic amongst the boys I'd missed, but now I could see it, in the hand signals and eye movements. Jacob was the leader of this little trio and Ethan would take the fall for his buddy.

"Jacob." I placed a hand on his shoulder. "Can I have a word?"

"Ethan told you. It's his," Jacob snapped, but rose to his feet anyway. He was taller than me and tried to use his height to intimidate. Silly child, did he think I'd never come across someone like him before? The pieces were falling into place and, despite Jacob's pleasant demeanor, I was beginning to suspect he was actually a bully.

"Sure," I drawled. "Next you'll be telling me you believe in Santa Claus and the Easter Bunny."

A flush of color crept up his neck. Swinging the backpack over one shoulder and hiding the wince at the weight, I crooked my finger at him. "Follow me."

Outside, I turned to the recalcitrant teen. "Tell me about the beer."

"It's Ethan's." He crossed his arms and glared at me.

"Oh, so this isn't the beer your uncle bought?" I eased the backpack off my shoulder and set it between my feet. Jacob didn't reply, but his expression had that *oh shit, I'm busted* look.

"Now why would your uncle buy you alcohol, hmmm? And why haven't you drunk it yet?"

"Okay fine!" His shoulders slumped and the swaggering demeanor vanished. "Uncle Dan bought me the beers. Me and the boys were going to go drinking out at the bluff, only Ryan's dad busted him sneaking out."

"When was this? The night Emily died?"

He nodded.

"So you weren't meeting her?"

"Nah. Things with Emily were..."

"What?"

"A little weird." This was the second time someone said Emily had been acting weird.

"In what way?"

"Like she wanted to be with me—when we were in public—but as soon as I got her alone she wasn't interested."

"Were you sleeping together?"

His cheeks burned bright red. He shook his head. "I wish. Like I said, she wasn't interested. I could hold her hand and kiss her in public and that was as far as she'd let me go. I thought she'd warm up to it, you know, but it'd been a couple of months and she still wasn't keen."

"Wait. A couple of months? You'd only been dating two months?"

"Two months is ages!" Jacob protested.

I rubbed my hand around the nape of my neck, my mind whirling. Emily had only been dating Jacob for two months and according to him they hadn't had sex. Emily had been twelve weeks pregnant. So there had to have been someone before Jacob. A secret boyfriend. But also, another niggling thought entered my brain.

"You weren't going to get her drunk, were you? Because it strikes me as strange that you'd go to all the trouble of buying beer and then not drink it."

"Told you, Ryan got caught sneaking out." Sarcasm dripped from every word. Rude little turd. I was starting to seriously dislike this teenager.

I curled my lip in a sneer. "You strike me as the type of dude who wouldn't pass up a good time just because one of his buddies got busted. I'd say you'd go right ahead and drink those beers yourself—or with Ethan. But you didn't. So.... that leaves me to speculate that you were planning on getting Emily drunk so she'd sleep with you—since she'd been turning down your advances consistently. Am I right, or am I right?"

Jacob blanched, and I shook my head. "Not cool, Jacob. Did your uncle know that's why you wanted the beer?"

"Please don't tell Uncle Dan." Jacob switched gears, widening his eyes and pleading. "He thought it was for a boys' night and he warned me it was a one off. He used to be wild in his youth and he knows dad and mom are so stiff."

"Stiff?"

"Straight-laced? Stuck up? By-the-book citizens who don't have any fun?"

"Ahh. Got it. Well, Jacob, sorry to be a party

pooper, but consider the beer confiscated."

"Doesn't matter." The swagger was back. "Sarah doesn't need any convincing to hang with me." He half tilted his head and laughed.

"So I hear. You been leading her on, Jacob? When Emily wouldn't put out, you made the moves on Sarah?"

"What? No way! She hit on me!"

Gosh, I couldn't keep up with these kids. "When was this?"

"The other night." He took a sudden interest in the tips of his shoes.

"The night Emily died, you mean?" Silence. "What happened?"

It came out in a rush. "I texted Emily to hang out, but as per usual, she brushed me off. Said she had something important to do. I had a six-pack of beer, so I texted Ryan and Ethan to meet up at the bluff. I was already on my way when I ran into Sarah. She lives around the corner from me. I turned on to her street and she was suddenly there, up in my business, brushing against me and asking if I wanted to, you know." He mimed squeezing a pair of boobs.

"And did you?"

He nodded, a gleam in his eye. "She kissed me," he said defensively, "and I kissed her back. She's hot, knows how to kiss. I was figuring me and her could drink the beer and, you know. And then she told me if I wanted to touch her anywhere else I had to dump Emily."

"But you didn't want to break up with Emily?" I wondered why. His behavior since Emily died didn't show he had any strong feelings for the dead girl. Why not dump her and hook up with her friend?

"It's all a game, you know? Emily'd been leading me on for weeks, thinking she's the boss of me. Sarah wasn't going to do the same. I mean, if she hadn't said that, hadn't ordered it, I probably would've done it anyway. I mean, why stay with Emily if Sarah was prepared to put out?"

What a gross little worm. "Then what happened?"

"Sarah didn't like it when I laughed and said no way. She got real mad. Slapped my face." He raised his hand to his cheek, probably remembering the sting. I wondered if Sarah was mad enough to confront Emily. To kill her. But Emily had been strangled, and that would take strength. But also, Emily possibly had a concussion and was in a weakened state, so she'd have been relatively easy to subdue.

"Get back inside," I told Jacob, pointing to the town hall. "And don't let me hear of you attempting to get a girl drunk again, or there will be consequences."

Without a word, Jacob spun on his heel and sauntered inside. I was pretty sure my threat didn't carry much weight with him, but I'd be having a word with his parents about his actions.

CHAPTER

TEN

" I wish we had popcorn."

"You're a ghost, you can't even eat popcorn."

Whitney crossed her arms and pouted, hovering in the armchair. She looked like she was sitting. Almost.

We'd reconvened at The Dusty Attic—Jenna, Monica, Gran, Jackson, and I—to update the murder board and discuss recent discoveries. I told them about the six-pack of beer I'd found in Jacob's bag.

"That makes sense," Monica announced. "I checked the records for the type of beer that Daniel bought. It stuck in my mind because it was unusual and we don't get a lot of it in. Actually, Harper, you may know it."

"Oh?"

"Grumpy's Brewhaus Adelaide Hills Pale Ale." She watched me expectantly, but I shrugged. Nope. It was new to me and I was pretty sure I'd remember a name like that. I hadn't seen the label on the beers in Jacobs backpack so I couldn't say for sure that was the brand of beer his uncle had bought for him.

"An Australian beer," Jenna said.

"You know it?"

She shook her head. "Mick might, but the important thing here is, is it the same brand that Jacob had in his bag?"

"Put it on the board, Mon," I told her. "It could come in handy."

"I wish I could still drink beer," Whitney said, giving up the pretense of sitting in the armchair. This time she drifted to the desk and perched—sort of—on the edge.

"Maybe you can." Gran grinned. "We could get you a bottle and you could submerge yourself in it."

Whitney looked hopeful. "Do you think that would work?"

"We should try it!" I could see where this was going. Gran was about to embark on a mission to get a ghost drunk. I had no idea if that was even possible, and no desire to find out.

"Ladies." Jackson rapped a knuckle on the murder board, drawing their attention back to the case at hand. "We've got work to do, remember?"

"Sorry," they said in unison and I bit back a grin.

"Let's go through our suspect list." I pointed to the first name on the board. "Hannah."

"The family's lawyer has requested we assess her for an impulse control disorder," Jackson told us. "Pyromania."

I nodded. "Makes sense. She's confessed to lighting the fires. And that she and Emily fought when Emily caught her trying to light a fire at the beach."

"It's confirmed the blood on the rock was Emily's," Jackson said. "But the ME doesn't believe the blow to the head killed her. Dazed, definitely."

"But Hannah ran off and didn't get help," Monica growled, her dark brows pulling together in a frown. "What sort of friend leaves a friend unconscious and bleeding and not help?"

"A scared one," Gran piped up. "Her life was unraveling. She knew lighting the fires was wrong but couldn't stop herself, couldn't control the compulsion. Her parents are right to get her assessed and get her the help she needs."

I pointed to the next post-it on the board. "What about Sarah? We know she has the hots for Jacob. Does she like him enough to kill the competition?"

"Her statement says she was home that night." Jackson had pulled up the notes he'd recorded on his phone.

"Wait." I frowned. "That's not true. She was out on

the street; Jacob ran into her. He lives just around the corner and he told me when Emily blew him off, he arranged to meet up with Ethan and Ryan at the bluff to drink the beers. On his way he ran into Sarah."

"So who is lying? Jacob or Sarah?" Jenna asked.

Gran snorted. "Probably both."

"Explain," Jackson requested.

"The two of them have some strange dynamic going on," Gran said. "She openly flirts, is overly suggestive with blatant sexual undertones in every interaction. He either pretends not to notice or makes a joke out of it. But his body language gives him away. He turns toward her whenever she's near. His hand will deliberately brush hers as he passes. There is more to those two, mark my words."

"He admitted that they kissed," I said. "He told me the night he ran into her she pushed up against him and kissed him and he didn't exactly fight her off."

Jackson typed a note in his phone. "I'll follow up with Sarah."

There was something in the glint of his eye, the way he held his shoulders and cocked his head ever so slightly. He noticed me noticing and gave a little shrug, then winked. And just like that, I was totally distracted.

"What about the other two? Ethan and Ryan. What's their relationship status?" Jenna asked.

"As in girlfriends?" Jackson asked, then answered without waiting for an answer. "Both unattached. The three of them have been friends since junior high."

"So they're tight. They'd lie for each other if they thought one of them was in trouble?" Jenna pushed.

"That's true. Ethan totally lied for Jacob when I busted them with the beer."

Monica sniggered. "So what you're saying here is that we have a bunch of suspects, all of them teenagers and all of them liars."

"Actually," Gran cut in, "I think Ryan is sweet on Hannah."

"Yeah, but he doesn't know she's a fire bug yet. That might change," I pointed out.

"We assume he doesn't know," Gran shot back. "Maybe he does."

"Okay, I know we're only speculating so let's just assume they're all lying. What do we know?" I stood in front of the board, sharpie and Post-its in hand.

"Emily was twelve weeks pregnant," Jackson supplied, "yet Jacob says they've only been together eight weeks." He nodded toward the board. "Query baby's father." I wrote it on a Post-it and stuck it to the board.

"The pregnancy... could that be the motive for murder? I mean, there are options for unwanted pregnancies." Jenna crossed her arms. As alarming as it was to consider someone had killed Emily because she was carrying a baby, we couldn't discount it.

"What about the phone?" I'd heard it ring from inside the locked beach hut.

"Waiting on the records from her provider, but definitely Emily's phone. It was under a bed. No signs of forced entry or a struggle so Emily must have had a key to let herself in."

"Or," Monica drawled, "the killer had a key and dragged her in there to kill her uninterrupted."

"We're dusting for prints. A lot depends on forensics."

"Is it possible that Emily and Jacob used to meet in the hut? That they used it for..." I paused and Monica filled in the silence, "For sex, you mean?"

"He told me they weren't sleeping together," I muttered.

"That girl was pregnant—she'd been sleeping with someone," Monica drawled. And once more we'd circled back to lying teenagers.

"Can we make them take a lie detector test?" I asked hopefully.

Jackson grinned. "It would be nice, but no." He ran a weary hand through his hair, then glanced at his watch. "It's getting late. I suggest we wrap this up for now."

"Hold on." Whitney had been remarkably silent

throughout our discussions. "You can see ghosts. Why not talk to Emily? Just ask her who killed her."

"I'm a necromancer, yes, but that doesn't mean I see or hear every dead person. If their spirit has crossed, I can't communicate with them. And don't think I haven't been keeping my eye out for her."

Whitney wrinkled her nose. "Can't I do it? I'm a ghost. It's only fair I should be able to see other ghosts."

"Have you tried?" he asked. "Maybe leave the store, go on an adventure."

"I can't leave the store," she huffed.

"Why not?"

"Because I died here. I'm stuck here."

He was shaking his head. "You're a ghost. A free spirit. You're only tied to the store because you think you are. Have you even tried to leave?"

What was he doing? It was bad enough that she was here, haunting my store, I didn't need to be bumping into her anywhere else. Although, maybe she'd go move in with Wendy and Bruce and bother them.

"But you and I control Whitney's presence," I pointed out. "She only appears when we're together."

"That's a phenomenon I've never encountered before." Jackson leaned back against the wall and crossed his arms over his chest. "And I have a theory."

"Oh?" Whitney hovered in front of him, eagerly waiting.

"I think it's all in your head," he said bluntly, eyeballing the ghost. "You were obsessed with Harper when you were alive, and your spirit has clung to that obsession, manifesting into this untrue belief you can only be present when she is here. It really has nothing to do with me per se."

Whitney's image shimmered and started to darken, something I'd never seen before. The lights overhead flickered.

"Uh-oh," Gran muttered. "Good one, Jackson, you've made her angry."

The whole room began to shake, books fell from the shelves and the lights continued to flicker.

"Enough!" Jackson said sternly, straightening and stepping forward until he was face-to-face with Whitney.

I swallowed. This was why I didn't like ghosts. They were scary. And Whitney right now was terrifying. Before she'd been pale, almost white, a semi-transparent being, but now she was dark, almost black, and looked exactly how I imagined the grim reaper to look, minus the scythe.

Even her voice was different, deep and low and it thundered around the room when she spoke. "That doesn't explain your role in this," she boomed.

"Calm. Down." Jackson ground out through a

clenched jaw. "Can't you see you're scaring her? Is that what you want? Was that your plan all along? Haunt Harper for the rest of her life?"

Whitney spun to look at me and I cringed, unable to stop the involuntary movement. Jackson was spot on, she was terrifying and any second now I'd pee my pants. I clamped my knees together just in case.

"Oh," Whitney said. And just like that, everything was back to normal. "I'm so sorry, Harper," she said, making a move toward me, but when I leaned away, she stopped and I slowly released the breath I didn't realize I'd been holding.

She turned her attention back to Jackson. "You must have a theory," she said calmly and sweetly, "as to why I appear when you're both here. You think I'm fixated on Harper, and fair call, maybe subconsciously I was. At the time of death, since I was handling the sale of The Dusty Attic, and I died here." She pointed to a spot on the floor and visions of the day I'd found her flitted through my mind.

I'd arranged to meet her here for the final handover of the keys after signing the contract earlier that day. She'd been flustered because she'd misplaced the keys so I'd agreed to meet her at the store. Whitney and I had never had much of a friendship when she was alive. She'd been my high school nemesis and when I'd returned to Whitefall Cove and purchased the store, dealing with her was a necessity, nothing more. Alive, Whitney had been a bully and a terror, steamrolling everyone to get what she wanted, only looking out for herself. In death? The exact opposite. It took some getting used to.

"I think I know." Monica was watching the drama unfold before her, her eyes darting from me, to Jackson, to Whitney before settling back on Jackson. "Jackson makes Harper feel safe. Hence, you, Whitney, only appear when he's with her so she isn't scared of you. Because that isn't your intent. If you wanted to scare her, you'd be here all the time, and you wouldn't limit yourself to the bookstore."

You could have heard a pin drop. Until Gran punctuated the silence with a fart. Jenna clapped her hand over her mouth, but a giggle escaped. Followed by another and soon she was bending forward, waves of laughter escaping her. Monica joined her and Jackson was trying to keep a straight face. I grinned. Trust Gran to break the ice by farting.

"That better not be a stink bomb," warned Monica with mock sternness. "My nose is far more sensitive than anyone else's here."

"Yeah, but you don't need to breathe, so just hold it," Gran shot back, unrepentant.

Jackson's phone vibrated, and he glanced at the screen before swiping to answer. "Ward." I watched as he listened intently to whoever was on the other end of the line. His eyes met mine. Something had happened. Something bad. His next words confirmed it. "I'll be right there." He hung up, then addressed the group.

"Sarah McClain is in the hospital. Attempted suicide."

The following morning I was surprised when Jordan showed up for work.

"Shouldn't you be at rehearsals?"

She shrugged, tossing her backpack beneath the desk, looking cool and casual in denim shorts and T-shirt. "Your Gran is over at the town hall arguing with Jacob's uncle about the booking."

I rolled my eyes. Gran was never one to back down from a confrontation, but what exactly were they arguing about? "The booking? For using the town hall you mean?"

She nodded. "Mr. Griffin says he has it booked for a fundraiser tonight and he needs early access to decorate. Gran isn't budging, saying she has it booked until five o'clock and he can go—"

I cut her off. "Got it." The talent competition was

tomorrow night, Gran needed all the rehearsal time she could get, although now she was another witch down I wondered if their performance would go ahead at all. "Have you heard how Sarah is?"

Jordan frowned, her face puzzled. "That was the weirdest thing, you know? Sarah is the last person I'd have thought would try to kill herself."

I had to agree. From what I'd seen and heard, Sarah was a confident young woman who didn't appear to have self-esteem issues. Goes to show you didn't really know what was going on in a person's life.

"But they say she's getting out of the hospital today." Jordan continued, "That she didn't take enough pills to actually die."

"Where did she get the pills from?" I'd waited up last night, hoping to hear from Jackson, but by midnight I'd given in and gone to bed. No word from him this morning, either, so I had no new information, and it was killing me not being in the loop. And okay, I was bummed he hadn't called or texted, not necessarily about the case, but just to say goodnight. Or good morning.

Jordan shrugged her shoulders. "Her mom, I think? Not that her mom gave them to her," she hastily added, "but that Sarah stole them from her mom's medicine cabinet."

Gran came bursting through the door, face flushed.

She pointed at Jordan. "To the town hall. We've only got this morning to prepare, every minute counts."

Dropping a kiss on Gran's cheek in greeting, I asked, "Reach a compromise with the councilman, did you?"

"Pft, darn politics," she grumbled, watching as Jordan collected her things. "Little upstart thinks he actually has a shot at being mayor."

"What about Sarah? You're another player down."

Gran grabbed my arm and leaned in close. "I heard she took her mom's Diazepam! But not enough to do any lasting damage. Pumped her stomach last night and discharging her this morning. She texted Hannah to say she's okay and will be fine for tomorrow night."

"Oh well, that's good. I'm glad she's okay."

Jordan hurried past us, breezily waving a hand in the air. "I'll see you in rehearsal, Mrs. B."

"Full dress rehearsal," Gran called after her, "the last one before the competition. We only have until lunchtime, but if you feel you need more time to memorize the routine, you and I can practice this afternoon."

Gran turned to me. "Councilman Griffin and I came to an agreement. He agreed to pay me a hundie to finish up by one o'clock."

"A hundie? As in... a hundred dollars?"

"Mmmhmmm." She winked. "He's desperate for

his fundraiser to be a success. Shoulda held out for more. I could probably have squeezed him up to two."

"I thought this was about the kids?" I teased.

She laughed. "That's the exact line I used!" Then she blew me a kiss and bustled out of the store. I watched her departing back, admiring her lack of inhibition when it came to her clothing choices. Today she was in hot pink fishnet tights, an orange tutu, and a WHAM T-shirt, knotted at the hem. On her wrists a multitude of neon bracelets. The tutu swished back and forth as she hurried down the sidewalk.

Flipping the sign from closed to open, I turned to put the coffee pot on and squealed when I nearly ran into Whitney. "Eeek!" Hand on my thumping heart I eyeballed the ghost who was hovering a foot away, a look of triumph on her face.

"I did it." She nodded in satisfaction.

"You sure did," I muttered darkly, not at all happy with this turn of events. "Have you tried leaving the bookstore? That might be a good idea."

"I did it," she said again, blinking at me.

"I heard you the first time."

"I did it."

"What's wrong with you?"

She moved toward me and I backed away. "Whitney, take it down a notch, would you?" But the ghost of Whitney Sims kept coming at me, repeating the words *I did it* like some sort of mantra.

I darted around her, moved behind the desk, but she just drifted right through the solid structure. Darn ghosts. Each time I moved away she followed, whatever I put in her path she moved right through, and I was on the verge of panicking when Jackson's voice rang out.

"Whitney!"

Both of us swiveled to see Jackson stagger out of the storeroom at the rear of the store. Had he been here the whole time?

"Oh." Whitney sighed in disappointment. She hadn't done it at all. She hadn't materialized without Jackson being present. I closed my eyes on a silent prayer of thanks. I wasn't sure I could cope with her ghost in my store twenty-four seven.

Then I noticed Jackson holding a hand to the back of his head.

"Are you okay?"

He pulled his hand away, and I saw blood. "Oh my God, you're hurt!" Rushing to his side I slung an arm around his waist to support him as he slumped. "What happened? How did you get in my store? How long have you been here?"

"I wish I could answer all those questions." He groaned, leaning heavily against me. "But I've got no idea. Last thing I remember is swinging by here last night to see if you were still here."

"Last night? You've been here all that time?" I

eased him into the chair behind the desk and pried his hand away from the wound on the back of his head. "Let me see."

I could see diddly squat except for blood matting his hair. "Wait here." Hurrying back into the storeroom, I retrieved the first aid kit, frowning at the small pool of blood on the floor. Someone attacked him and left him for dead. In my store. None of it made sense.

Swiveling the chair so he was facing me, I pressed a gauze pad against the wound with one hand, and touched his cheek with the other. He had a lovely gray pallor going on.

"I think I should call an ambulance," I said. He shook his head, then winced at the movement.

"No. Call the station." He patted his pockets, searching for his phone. "Darn." He cursed.

"Whoever did this took your phone?" I guessed. He nodded, then groaned.

"Stop moving your head. Here, hold this, and stop moving. You've probably got a concussion." Once he had a grip on the gauze, I grabbed my phone and dialed, delighted when the dulcet tones of Officer Liliana Miles answered.

"Whitefall Cove Police."

"This is Harper Jones. I'm at The Dusty Attic with Detective Ward. He's injured."

"Injured? How?"

"I don't know. I found him like this. A head injury, a blow to the back of the head by the looks of things."

"Oh, so you're a detective now?" Her voice dripped sarcasm and I could picture her in my mind, complete with eye roll.

Jackson overheard and took the phone from me. "Liliana," he snapped, "either send someone else or come yourself. I don't care which, but I want this place dusted for prints. Someone jumped me out front last night and dragged me in here."

"Hadn't you better get checked out then?" she shot back.

"I will. As soon as a squad gets here Harper's taking me to the hospital." He looked at me and I nodded. Fine with me. I crossed to the front door and flicked the sign back to closed. Jackson finished the call and closed his eyes, the phone sliding from his fingers to the desk with a soft thud.

"Jackson?" Rushing to his side, I was relieved when his eyes opened and he gave me a grin.

"Sorry, didn't mean to scare you. I've got the mother of all headaches."

"You said someone jumped you. Out front?"

"Yeah. Probably around eleven thirty. I only stopped because it was on the way home from the hospital and despite it being an extreme long shot I figured, what the hell, you might still have been here working on the murder board. Plus, I wanted to see you."

My heart warmed. I'd wanted to see him too.

"I couldn't see any lights, but I got out and checked the door, more out of habit to check it was secure than anything else."

"And someone hit you?"

"I heard a sound behind me, and before I could turn, it was boom, lights out."

The screech of tires outside heralded a patrol car and my shoulders slumped when Liliana herself banged on the door. Opening the door I stepped aside as she strode inside. Setting a forensic case at her feet, she studied Jackson for a moment before turning her attention to me.

"You'd better get him to the hospital. He's not looking so hot."

I nodded, slung my bag over my shoulder, and slid my arm around Jackson's waist to help him out of the chair.

"If you leave before I get back, will you lock the door? Please," I asked as we shuffled past her.

"Affirmative." She'd turned her attention to the task at hand, snapping on latex gloves.

"I'll see you back at the station," Jackson told her.

She paused, frowning. "It would be faster if someone came to the hospital and got your statement. They will hold you for observation at the very least."

A silent battle went on between them, his green eyes locked on her hazel one's, neither blinking. It went on for so long I wondered if they were communicating telepathically, if that was even possible between a necromancer and a fae, when Jackson suddenly blinked.

"Whatever." He straightened up, and keeping the gauze pressed to his skull, led the way outside. I followed silently.

The drive to the hospital was equally silent. Jackson's color hadn't improved, and he staggered when he climbed out of the car.

"I've got you." Sliding my arm around his waist, I knew he was holding back, trying not to lean on me. "Jackson. You can lean on me. I won't break."

He snorted. "You have no idea how heavy I am. I'd crush you." I eyed his six-foot-four frame.

"Yeah okay, you can lean on me a little," I amended.

He didn't lean on me at all, but slung an arm around my shoulders to keep me close. It was nice. If only he weren't bleeding from a severe head wound, it would have been downright romantic.

A triage nurse glanced up when we entered and, recognizing Jackson, hurried forward.

"What's happened, Detective?" she asked, vetoing the waiting room and guiding us straight into the treatment area.

"A run-in with a blunt object." Jackson grinned, lifting the blood-soaked gauze to show her.

She made a tsk sound. "Let's get that cleaned up and take a look. Did you lose consciousness at all?"

"I think so. I don't remember."

"He was on the floor of my store all night," I told the nurse. "They attacked him outside and whoever did it dragged him into my store and left him in the storage room. I didn't know he was there until he staggered out this morning."

Seating Jackson on a gurney, she helped him lie back, then shone a light in his eyes, studying his pupils. "That's a long time to be unconscious," she said, then, satisfied with the results of her eye exam, she turned to look at me. "We will be awhile. He will need an x-ray, possibly a CT scan to make sure there's no bleeding on the brain." She turned his head and examined the wound. "Not severe. Might need a stitch or two. Head wounds bleed like crazy, making them look worse than they are."

I looked at Jackson's prone form. His eyes were closed against the glare of the overhead light and his skin still had an unhealthy pallor. I was reasonably sure they'd admit him, even if it was only for observation. Nodding to the nurse, I touched Jackson's hand, leaning over so my mouth was close to his ear.

"I'm going to visit Sarah since I'm here. I'll check back in a little while, okay?"

"About that," he murmured, keeping his voice low, "I don't believe Sarah attempted suicide. I think she was dosed."

I reared back. "Dosed? How?"

"Alcohol. Beer. I'm waiting on lab results on the type of beer, but I suspect—"

"Grumpy's Brewhaus?"

He nodded. "They pumped Sarah's stomach when she was brought in. After interviewing her family and friends I'm confident she's not suicidal, but someone wanted it to look that way. I suspect they added the pills to the beer."

"I'll see if I can find out who she was drinking with." I softly pressed my lips to his cheek. "Stay out of trouble."

He chuckled. "Likewise, Jones." He gave me a wink, then closed his eyes again. The nurse hustled me out of the way to check his blood pressure and I slowly backed away, losing sight of him when another nurse arrived and whipped the curtain around the treatment bay closed.

Pulling out my phone, I headed toward the elevator. Sarah would be on a ward on the third floor. I pulled up Jenna's number as I stepped inside.

"Morning, Harper," she answered on the second ring.

"Morning, Jenna. Hey, quick question, if someone's phone is stolen, is there a way to find it? Track it?"

"There's a 'find my phone' app that could do it," she replied, "But the app has to be installed in the first place, and the stolen phone would have to be turned on for it to work. Why?"

I filled her in on what had happened with Jackson and how his phone appeared to be missing.

"Well, that is the most bizarre thing I've ever heard." I could picture her in my mind's eye, leaning back in her chair and staring up at the ceiling. "So someone knocked him out, then went to the trouble of breaking into your store, dragging him not only inside but all the way to the storeroom, left him there, and locked up behind themselves."

"And took his phone."

"And took his phone," she repeated. "His phone would be police issue, their IT department can easily trace it, but again, it would have to be on for that to work. And if you stole a cop's phone you'd have gotten what you want from it and then would either dump it or turn it off and leave it off."

"It's weird, huh?" The elevator arrived at the third floor and I stepped out, heading to the nurse's station.

"I wonder if it's related," she muttered, more to herself than to me.

"Related to what?"

"I've been doing more digging," she admitted, "into Blake, and why he was here."

I snorted. "He was here to defend Gran."

"Yes, I know, but why would a partner in a law firm come all this way to defend an open and shut case? We all knew that Gran didn't do it and it would be relatively easy for any lawyer to represent her—it wasn't a complex case."

"Yeah, but he's also friends with my dad. That's probably why." It was the reason I'd settled on, since initially I couldn't work out why a lawyer of Blake's caliber would come to small town Whitefall Cove for such a case either.

"Now that I know about the Bureau of Occult Research and Defense, and the Tennant family ties to it, it got me thinking..."

"And?"

"Well, with a little help from Remy, we discovered that Blake had other business in Whitefall Cove," she said.

"Oh? Do you know what?"

"Only that he was investigating someone. I don't know who yet. Remy can only help me so much. I don't want her to get in trouble with the Bureau."

I digested what she'd just told me. "Correct me if I'm wrong," I began, "but you're saying that whatever Blake was doing in Whitefall Cove, it could involve Jackson? That's why he was attacked?"

"Not directly. Look, Harper, I'm just thinking out loud. Jackson is a detective, he records statements and case notes directly into his phone, and if Blake is doing clandestine assignments for the Bureau, then... I don't know. It could be related, maybe it isn't."

Reaching the nurse's station, I put a hand over the phone and asked for Sarah's room number. Smiling my thanks, I headed down the corridor.

"Blake wouldn't hurt Jackson though. Would he?" I returned to the call with Jenna.

"I don't think that's Blake's style. And he had plenty of opportunity to confront Jackson while he was in town, so no, I don't think he's behind Jackson's attack per se."

"But?"

"Maybe they were looking into the same thing?"

"But Jackson is looking into Emily's murder. Blake was here weeks before that even happened."

"You're right. I'm grasping at straws." She sighed.

"No, you've got exceptional instincts." I froze, a thought solidifying in my brain. "You could be right. What if, as part of Jackson's investigation, he's stumbled upon the same person who Blake was here to investigate? And that person is uber paranoid?"

"They're not a killer though," Jenna pointed out. "It would have been far easier to kill Jackson, instead they dragged him into your store."

I gasped. "To frame me?"

"Possibly."

I'd reached the door to Sarah's room. "I gotta go. I'm still at the hospital. I'm checking in on Sarah while I wait for them to do x-rays and stuff on Jackson."

"Call me when you're done, okay?"

"Will do." Hanging up, I pushed the door open. Sarah was asleep, her mother, Kristin, was slouched in an armchair in the corner. Hearing the door open, she glanced up, then lifted her finger to her lips to shush me so as not to wake her daughter. She indicated she'd come out, so I backed up and waited in the corridor for her.

"Hi, Kristin, how you holding up?"

She looked exhausted, and I assumed she'd spent the night by her daughter's side.

"I'm beat." She sighed. "Thanks for dropping by," she continued, "but it's a little early for visiting hours isn't it?"

"Oh, I was here anyway." I shrugged. "I thought I'd swing by and see how she's doing. Gran says she's okay?"

Kristin's shoulders slumped and her eyes filled with tears.

"Oh hey, sorry, I didn't mean to upset you!" Wrapping an arm around the other woman's shoulders, I steered her away from Sarah's room. "Let's go grab a coffee, hmm?" I'd spied a vending machine a little further along the corridor.

Dragging a worn tissue from her jeans pocket, Kristin wiped her nose and gave me a watery smile.

"Sorry," she sniffed, "I'm an emotional wreck. I just never thought this could happen to my kid, you know? I'm a teacher, I'm trained to look for the signs and I never saw that my own kid was hurting so much she'd try to take her own life."

"Wait, Kristin." I peered at her in puzzlement. "Has no one told you?"

"Told me what?"

I bit my lip. Jackson had told me he didn't think Sarah had tried to kill herself, but maybe that wasn't common knowledge. Still, I couldn't keep such a thing from the girl's own mother.

"Look, the police will talk to you about this, but here's what I've heard. They don't think Sarah tried to kill herself. Hasn't Sarah talked to you? Told you what happened?"

"She doesn't remember." Kristin wiped at her face. "Not a thing. But how do you know?"

"Because Detective Ward told me. Just now. He's in being treated for an injury and I said I'd pop in to see Sarah while I'm waiting. But look, I'm sure once he's done in emergency, he'll come and talk to you himself."

Buying us both a coffee I handed one to Kristin, then we slowly walked back to Sarah's room. "They think Sarah's drink was roofied."

Kristin paled. "But... they said she took Diazepam. That she stole it from my medicine cabinet."

"The Diazepam was taken with alcohol. Beer. And I'd assume you're not the only one in Whitefall Cove who takes Diazepam. Have you checked your prescription to see if any are missing?"

"Beer? Sarah doesn't drink. She's seventeen for Pete's sake!" I remembered sneaking a bottle of vodka from my parent's stash and getting drunk one night with Monica and Jenna when I was sixteen. Teenagers most certainly did drink, like it or not.

"Do you know what she was doing last night? Did she go out? Did she meet up with friends?"

Another tear slid down her cheek. "She doesn't tell me anything anymore. It's so hard being a single mom. I've tried to bring her up to be confident and independent and know that she can have anything she wants as long as she puts her mind to it. Yet now she sneaks out, lies."

"Has she mentioned Jacob Griffin to you at all?"

"His name came up when your Gran first started the lessons for the talent competition. She was angry she hadn't been paired with him, said she'd only joined up to be with him and that she got stuck with Ethan instead. Is this all to do with him?"

I shrugged. "It's best you ask Sarah about that." I wasn't about to fill her mother in on her seduction attempts on Jacob. "Can you tell me about last night? What happened?"

"I thought she was in her room. I'd told her she

wasn't going out in the evening, not alone, not with Emily's killer on the loose. If she wanted to go somewhere, I'd drive her and pick her up. She'd stormed off and I could hear her music playing so I figured she was sulking. Then her favorite show came on and I know she loves to watch it, so I knocked on her door to let her know. When she didn't answer I let myself in. She wasn't there, she'd snuck out, left her window open to get back in."

"You didn't go looking for her?"

"I thought about it. But then I thought I'd watch the soap myself, and then I'd go find her and ground her for sneaking out." The tears were flowing freely now. "Next thing I know the police are at the door saying they had found her unconscious on the beach from an overdose."

Sobs wracked through her body, shaking her frame, and I pulled her into my arms, rubbing a soothing hand up and down her back. I couldn't imagine how awful it must be for her. Once the storm had passed, she eased out of my embrace, eyes red. "Sorry."

"Don't be. What happened to Sarah was truly awful."

"Do you think," she sniffed, "do you think whoever killed Emily did this? Did they try to kill my little girl?"

"I honestly don't know," I admitted. But it was a totally different MO. Emily had been strangled.

Someone had drugged Sarah in an attempt to make it look like suicide. The two girls knew each other, were best friends, so I had to assume the attack on Sarah was related. But who? Who could get close enough to her to drug her?

CHAPTER
TWELVE

When I returned to check on Jackson in emergency, they wouldn't let me see him, saying he was still having tests and they'd call me. Unable to concentrate and not relishing sitting in the waiting room for hours on end, I decided to drop in on Gran and see how rehearsals were progressing.

I'd pulled up out front and had just locked my car when I saw Daniel Griffin talking to the driver of a small truck.

"Hey!" I shouted, heading toward them, "I want a word with you."

Daniel finished signing a piece of paper on a clipboard, handed it back to the driver, and turned to face me.

"Harper. What can I do for you? I don't have much

time. Kinda busy here today. The deliveries are arriving for the fundraiser." He nodded toward the truck. The driver had opened the rear doors and lifted down a trolley. Boxes of wine were stacked in the back.

"Actually, that's what I wanted to talk to you about." I gestured toward the wine and he cocked a brow.

"Wine?"

"Not wine exactly. Beer. Do you know how irresponsible it is to supply minors with alcohol? Let alone illegal?"

He folded his arms across his chest and looked down his nose at me. "Not you too. I've already told that reporter friend of yours and I'll tell you too. I do not supply minors with alcohol."

I snorted. "Yeah, sure. That's not what your nephew says."

"Jacob?" His arms dropped, and he looked genuinely surprised.

"Do you have any other nephews?"

He dragged in a breath, then blew it out slowly before running a hand around the back of his neck, muttering beneath his breath, "That kid will be the death of me." Straightening, he said to me, "Look, I don't know what Jacob's told you, but I suspect it wasn't the truth."

"So he's lying?"

"Most likely. What's this all about?"

"Jacob told me you were the one who supplied him with beer. The night Emily died, he and his mates were drinking."

A flush of color darkened his cheeks and his eyes narrowed. "I assure you, I did no such thing."

"Can you explain then, why you did in fact buy a six-pack of Grumpy's Brewhaus beer from Brewed Awakening? Especially since you don't drink beer."

"Been doing your research, I see," he grumbled, glancing at the delivery guy who trundled past us with three boxes of wine on his trolley.

"Avoiding the question?"

He leaned in close, so close I could see the flecks of gold in his brown eyes. "Not that it is *any* of your business..." His breath blew hot on my face and a shiver danced up my spine. I held my ground, refusing to be intimidated by him, despite him towering over me. "But I purchased that beer for a private dinner in my home. One of my guests—a potential donor to my campaign—is partial to it. As a matter of fact, I've got six cases in the back of this truck." He waved a hand at the truck beside us. "Shall we check it's all present and accounted for and I haven't siphoned any of it off for my wayward nephew?"

"Probably unnecessary," I demurred. His story sounded plausible. We were leading into an election, it only made sense he'd be doing a lot of entertaining and schmoozing.

"Why would Jacob tell me you bought it for him?" I wondered out loud.

"Because he's a teenager." Daniel huffed, taking a step back, giving me room to breathe. "And all they think about is getting laid and making stupid decisions. Girls. Cars. Beer." He ticked off on his fingers. "I should know, I was a teenager once." He cocked his head. "Are you sure it was Jacob who had the beer in the first place? It could have been Ethan or Ryan, they're as thick as thieves."

"I found it in Jacob's backpack."

"Pretty damning then." Daniel shook his head. "Look, I have an idea. We can go to my place and see if the six-pack is still there. I left it in the bar fridge. If it's still there, well, obviously that isn't where the beer Jacob had in his possession came from. But if it's missing? Then I need to have a stern word with my nephew."

Seeing my hesitation, he touched my shoulder and gave me a smile and I could see why he was in politics. He was charismatic and full of charm—when he wanted to be. "My house is one block over. Literally a two-minute walk. I'll have you back in no time, I swear."

I considered him for another second or two, then shrugged. "Okay then." What did I have to lose? Nothing. If the beer was still in Daniel's bar fridge, then Jacob was clearly lying. And if it wasn't, then I had to decide who was telling the lie. Daniel, about his nephew stealing it, or Jacob, about his uncle supplying it.

True to his word, the walk to his house took mere minutes. Only it wasn't a house, but an apartment, but prime location and beautifully appointed.

"Nice place," I said, waiting while he unlocked the padlock on the front gate. I followed him down the path to the front door.

"Yep, not too shabby." He agreed, unlocking the front door and ushering me ahead of him. The inside of his apartment was tastefully decorated in art deco style. "This is just a stopgap. I've got my eye on the mayor's house."

"Ahh." I nodded. The mayor's house came with the job and was located in beautifully manicured gardens along the esplanade.

"Come on up." Daniel stood at the bottom of the stairs. "The formal living room is up here, best views."

He wasn't wrong. A plush white sofa dominated the space, tossed on one end was the pinstripe suit jacket he'd worn the night of the fire, the presumably silk tie thrown on top. I took a step closer, eyeing the tie thoughtfully. It would make a handy weapon to strangle someone with. From the floor-to-ceiling windows I could see the park across the road, and on an angle, the mayor's house and beach beyond. He *literally* had an eye on the mayor's house.

While I stood in thought, Daniel crossed to the bar and opened the fridge. "Well, I'll be damned."

"What?" I turned, and he stood back so I could see the contents. No beer.

"Darn it. I was hoping to avoid this." Daniel pursed his lips, then looked at me.

"What?"

"Let me check something first. I'm hoping I'm wrong." I followed him into his study where he pulled a book from the bookshelves and flipped it open. Ah, it was actually a box disguised to be a book.

"Oh, Jacob." Daniel turned and showed me the box. Inside were a handful of keys, each on its own key tag. I looked from the keys to Daniel, brows raised.

"The key to the beach hut is missing. This is where I keep it. I'd meant to check earlier, but things have been pretty hectic with the fundraiser coming up and it slipped my mind."

"Does Jacob know you keep the key there? And what are the other keys for... if you don't mind me asking."

"A spare house key, the spare key to my parents' place, key for my office, some old keys I don't even know what they belong to." He shrugged. "Look, I hate to say this, I was hoping against hope to give my wayward nephew the benefit of the doubt, but this isn't the first time he's done something like this."

"Like what?"

"Stealing. Drinking. Sex."

"Oh?"

"Last year he stole a bottle of scotch from his parents. Went drinking with a girl, one thing led to another, only after, when they were both sober, he realized it was a mistake, only she wanted more and it was all messy for a while."

"Who was the girl?"

He tapped a finger against his lips, eyes studying the carpet. Then he snapped his fingers. "Anna? Or Hannah? Something like that. The pretty blonde with the unusual gray eyes. She's in the talent show with him."

"Hannah Burton?" I blinked in surprise. I'd seen Hannah and Jacob together and hadn't picked up any vibes that the two of them had once had a thing.

"I guess. I don't really know all their names— something I should remedy I guess. After all, they're going to be voting age soon." He flashed his white teeth, all polished politician. "I hope this has been of some help, Harper?" He guided me out of the office and back down the stairs. "But I really need to be getting back."

"It has. Thanks."

"And rest assured I will be speaking with Jacob about this. He has a family name to represent and I will not tolerate this sort of behavior. Maybe it's time to speak to his parents about boarding school." The last was more to himself than to me, and I remained silent as we headed back to the town hall, each lost in our own thoughts.

We arrived at the same time as Sarah and her mom.

"Oh, hi guys." I waved, crossing to them as Daniel headed back to the delivery driver who was finishing up.

"I didn't expect to see you here so soon." I touched Sarah's arm in a friendly gesture and she smiled, pale, but her violet eyes hadn't lost their sparkle.

"Sarah insisted on coming. But no rehearsal, just to touch base with her friends and then we're going home to rest."

"Yes, Mom." Sarah rolled her eyes. "I told you, I'm fine." She strolled ahead of us into the hall. Watching her, you wouldn't have thought she'd had her stomach pumped the night before.

"Is she okay?" I kept my voice low so she wouldn't overhear. Kristin looked in a worse condition than her daughter, drawn and haggard.

"She's actually right." Kristin snorted. "She's fine. They discharged her not long after your visit. Said that after they'd pumped her stomach, they probably didn't have to, that she hadn't taken that many pills, just enough to knock her out. No lasting damage."

"Well, that's good news. So..." I hesitated for a

second. "You said that she hadn't taken that many. Have the police spoken to you yet?"

Kristin shook her head. "No, but after that news, I think she was definitely roofied. I just haven't mentioned it to Sarah yet. Because whoever did this, she knows them. Trusts them. The doctors told me she may experience flashes of memory, but not to force it, so until she remembers who she was with, I'm sticking close. Trust no one."

I chewed on my lip. I could see Kristin's point of view, wanting to protect her daughter, but with her daughter not knowing someone had done this to her intentionally, her guard would be down.

Seeing my hesitation, Kristin grabbed my wrist. "Please don't say anything. I've got this. I've been solely responsible for Sarah her entire life. I know my daughter. It's best she doesn't know."

I nodded. Fair enough. It wasn't my decision to make. Although I still thought it was the wrong one. We followed Sarah inside and I watched as the kids finished up. They looked amazing. Ethan was temporarily partnered with Gran as they went through their final routine. Daniel stood leaning against a wall, watching, but constantly checking his watch.

Sarah clapped in delight when the routine finished and the team lowered themselves to the floor. "You guys, that was incredible! It looks even more amazing watching from the floor."

"Hey, Sarah." Hannah beamed. Hiking up her ball gown skirts, she hurried over to hug her friend. "How are you feeling? Are you okay?"

"I'm fine, honestly. And, Mrs. B, I will be here tomorrow night, I swear."

"It's good to see you, Sarah love." Gran approached, still dressed in her tutu, and gave Sarah a hug. "Now tell us, we're dying to know, what happened? Got into your mom's booze, did you?"

Kristin stiffened by my side and I shot Gran a warning glare, but Sarah handled the query with aplomb. "Actually, I don't know," she admitted. "The doctors tell me I have some form of amnesia."

"Really?" Jacob asked, eyes wide. "You don't remember anything? At all?"

She shook her head. "Nope. Last thing I remember is listening to music in my bedroom. I have no idea how I got to the beach."

"Wow. That's rad." Ethan and Ryan said in unison. Kristin snapped her gaze to them, and, noticing her glare, Ethan hurriedly amended their statements. "I mean weird. That's weird. But glad you're okay, Sarah." Ethan gave her a wink. "Not that I didn't appreciate Mrs. B being my partner."

Gran grinned. "Okay, kids. That's a wrap. Mister 'I've got the hall booked and can't wait for you lot to get out so I can decorate' is keen for us to leave. The show starts tomorrow at seven; I want you here at five. Got it?"

"Yes, Mrs. B," they chorused.

"Jordan, you and I will put in some extra time. You've picked up most of the routine, just a couple of rough spots. I think if we go over it one more time— maybe two—you'll be solid."

"Is that okay, Harper?" Jordan asked. "Who's looking after the store?"

"It's closed at the moment." I motioned the two of them to follow me away from the group.

"What's happened?" she asked. I filled them in on finding Jackson injured in the store.

"That's so weird." Jordan gasped, hand over her mouth. "Who would do that?"

"Very good question. I have no idea."

CHAPTER
THIRTEEN

I watched as Jordan and Gran headed off to an apparently secret location to continue practicing for tomorrow night's competition. Hannah stood nearby, chewing on a fingernail. The boys had cleared out, no doubt off to play video games. I'd overheard them fanatically fanboying over some game called Fortnite.

"Hey, Hannah, is someone picking you up?"

She jumped when I approached and quickly pulled her finger from her mouth.

"Yeah. Mom is. She's just finishing up with a client."

"Must be busy at the salon?"

Hannah shrugged. "I guess. Mostly blow outs for the dinner tonight." She nodded at the town hall where a stream of people were carrying boxes inside, ready to set up for the big event.

"How are you holding up?"

"Okay." She kept her eyes on her shoes and scuffed a toe on the ground.

"So you and Jacob are good friends?"

Her eyes darted my way. "I guess."

"I didn't know you and he had a thing."

"We didn't."

"Oh? I heard you and he hooked up last year?"

Color flooded her cheeks, and she folded her arms across her chest. "We didn't. We got drunk and passed out. Nothing happened. Despite that moron running around telling everyone he'd scored."

"Ohhhhh," I said in sympathy. "That sucks. Why do boys do that?"

"Because they're jerks," she muttered.

"They can be." I remembered my fair share of jerks when I'd been in school. "I'm glad your parents didn't make you pull out of the competition." I changed the subject, although it probably wasn't a safer topic.

She shrugged. "I am grounded. But it's school vacation and they're both working. So basically the rehearsals are their way of knowing where I am and what I'm doing. Now I get to go to the salon and sweep the floor all afternoon." Her voice cracked and her chin wobbled.

Wrapping an arm around her shoulders, I squeezed her tight. "Things will work out."

A car pulled to the curb, and the window rolled down.

"Come on, Hannah!" Jacqueline Burton yelled. "I've got Mrs. Evans in for a cut and color any minute."

"See you," Hannah said to me and hurried over to slide into the passenger seat.

"Bye." I lifted a hand to wave, watching as the car pulled out and zipped off down Main Street.

Despite Hannah lighting the fires, I felt for her. And her parents. I couldn't imagine the pain they must be going through. It was a sorry situation all the way around, but hopefully Hannah getting caught was a wake-up call to them all.

Shaking off the maudlin thoughts, I glanced at the time. Midday. No word from Jackson, but then he was minus his phone, so I decided I'd check on him, see if they'd admitted him or not.

Turned out they hadn't. He was still on the gurney where I'd left him in the treatment bay. The curtain around his bed was pulled back giving me a clear view of him sitting up, the color back in his face.

"Oh hey," he greeted me warmly. "Glad you're back. I'm about to get discharged."

"You are? So, no concussion?"

"Oh, he has a concussion all right!" The same nurse who'd tended to him when I first brought him in bustled over. "And we will discharge him provided he has someone with him at all times for the next twelve hours."

"Oh well, I can do that?" I offered.

"Perfect. I'll get the paperwork sorted." She hurried away again, and I frowned at Jackson.

"But you were unconscious all night? Why would they discharge you?"

"Because I wasn't really unconscious. Well, I was, briefly, but I have no signs of brain injury or a bleed on the brain—they think I slept it off, that I wasn't unconscious all that time, just asleep. Concussions make you drowsy, so by the time you found me, I was over the worst. And now I have some pain killers onboard, I'm good to go."

I sagged in relief. That was excellent news. Seeing my face, Jackson grabbed my hand. "Sorry I gave you such a fright."

"Well, just try not to do it again, okay?" Leaning forward, I kissed his cheek, and he was reaching up to touch my face when we were interrupted by a commotion from behind.

I turned to see Jacob's parents, Jeremy and Kathleen, marching into the emergency department, Jacob trailing behind them. With the curtains open around Jackson's treatment bay we had a clear view as the trio made their way to the reception desk. Jeremy was arguing with someone on the phone and Jackson and I watched—and listened—with interest.

"I don't care what you think," Jeremy snapped into the phone. "This is not your decision and Jacob is not your son." Silence as he listened to whoever was on the other end of the call. "Absolutely not. You're obsessed with your career and public image, Dan. This is my child we're talking about and submitting to a DNA sample will clear his name. He did not hurt that girl. This will prove it. No, I don't care what your lawyer says. Stay out of it." He jabbed at the screen, disconnecting the call. Running a hand through his hair, he approached the reception desk.

"Yes, I was told to report here for a DNA test for my son, Jacob Griffin."

"Thanks for coming in, Mr. Griffin." Liliana Miles appeared from nowhere, as she had a habit of doing, and I stiffened. Jackson squeezed my hand, but I didn't take my eyes off the scene unfolding before me. "The test is a simple swab from the inside of his cheek. The nurses will do it. I'm just here to witness it to maintain the chain of evidence."

"Fine. Let's get this over with."

Liliana swung around and her eyes landed on me, then Jackson. Nothing. Her face revealed nothing. Turning back to the Griffin family, she said, "The nurse will be with us shortly. Take a seat." Then headed our way. I'm pretty sure my gulp was audible, and Jackson again squeezed my hand.

"How are you feeling?" Liliana asked him as she stood at the foot of his bed.

"Fine. About to be discharged. How's the case?"

"The Griffins' beach hut has DNA evidence that Emily was inside. Hair, fingerprints, bodily fluids."

Bodily fluids? As in? Ewww. So Emily had been having sex in the hut with Jacob.

"The family has agreed to a DNA sample. The boy swears he has never had intercourse with her, therefore the DNA we found can't belong to him."

Jackson nodded. "Best way to rule him out then."

"Yeah, but Jacob stole the key from his uncle," I said.

Liliana's eyes zeroed in on me, cold as steel. "He also denies that. Just because the key is missing doesn't mean Jacob took it."

"She's right." Jackson nodded. To Liliana he said, "Anything else? Do we have the phone records yet?"

"Came in this morning. Philips is going over them."

The nurse who'd treated Jackson shot past to where the Griffin family waited. "Looks like we're up," Liliana said, spinning on her heel and stalking away.

"This should wrap up the case," Jackson murmured, watching them follow the nurse into a treatment room. "Prove Jacob is the baby's father and that he was with her in the hut."

"The timeline doesn't match up though," I pointed out. "Emily was already pregnant when she and Jacob started dating. Plus Jacob's uncle owns the hut, it's feasible that his DNA would be there."

"Let's wait and see what the test results reveal."

I thought about the tie I'd seen in Daniel's house. "Do they know what was used to strangle Emily?"

"Initially, we thought maybe a belt, but that would have left harsh welts in her skin. The ME thinks a fabric, soft. They pulled a fiber that we're hoping to identify."

"A fiber? Like... from a tie?"

He nodded. "Possibly. Or a scarf. Or stockings. Even a T-shirt or hand towel." His brows pulled together in a frown, but then he looked at me and the lines eased. "So, looks like we're going to be hanging out for a while." His grin was cheeky and endearing.

"Guess so," I drawled, as if having to keep an eye on him was the biggest burden in the world.

While we waited for the nurse to return I filled him in on the morning's discoveries and my chat with Daniel Griffin.

"I assume that was Daniel that Jeremy was arguing with on the phone when they came in." My eyes drifted over to the closed door where Jacob was having a DNA swab.

"Well, he did say Dan, so yeah, good call, Sherlock." Jackson was sitting on the edge of the bed, his legs dangling over the side. I slapped his knee.

"Police brutality now, Jones?" One dark brow arched and the twinkling was back in his eyes.

"You wish." Shoving my hands into the back pockets of my jeans, I shifted my weight from foot to foot, growing impatient at the wait. And finding it harder by the minute to keep my hands to myself. It was safer if they stayed tucked away in my pockets.

"Whatever you're thinking"—his voice dropped to a deep growl that sent shivers of anticipation dancing across my skin—"I like it."

My eyes met his in a clash of emotion. Want, desire, but also a touch of fear. The feelings I had for Jackson were multiplying rapidly, and the sudden realization that if this didn't work out with us, if he decided I was damaged goods after all, the pain that would follow would be unimaginable. Not to mention I'd lose him as a friend. He saw it. The second the thought entered my head, he saw the change, the slight stiffening of my body, the narrowing of my eyes, the way my heart rate spiked and then dropped back into rhythm.

His growl was more pronounced as his hand shot out and seized mine. "Don't. You went someplace you didn't have to."

"But—"

"Harper," he said, my name coming out on a sigh, tugging me closer so I was wedged in between his knees, "don't borrow trouble. We've waited this long, let's just enjoy the moment, enjoy each other, hmmm?"

My breath hitched in my throat. Being this close to him, I could barely think, let alone worry about what the future might hold. I was leaning in, drawn to him like a moth to a flame, when the nurse who had been treating him earlier appeared.

"You're free to go," she said. "Remember, take it easy. No physical activity." Her eyes darted between us, her meaning clear. My cheeks heated with color, but Jackson just chuckled, his smirk revealing the dimple that melted women's hearts.

"Way to kill the mood." He winked at her and she smiled back, handed him a pamphlet on head injuries and things to look out for, and was then ushering us out the door, declaring she had other patients that needed her attention.

"Your place or mine?" Jackson rested his hand on the nape of my neck as we headed toward my car in the parking lot.

"I thought for sure you'd play the tough guy and insist on working," I admitted.

"Police regulations. I'm not cleared for duty until" —he glanced at a slip of paper I hadn't noticed before —"eight a.m. tomorrow."

"Oh."

"But that doesn't mean I won't be working." He rubbed his thumb up and down the side of my neck, distracting me. "I'll just be doing it with you in the comfort of your home. Or mine. I'm easy. In fact, I think I will enjoy this enforced sick leave."

CHAPTER
FOURTEEN

We ended up back at my place because of Archie. I'd left him at home this morning and if my day had panned out the way I'd expected it to, I'd been intending to drop in at lunchtime and take him back to the Dusty Attic with me. Of course none of that had happened so now it was midafternoon and I was worried about the state of my house from a bored and neglected feline. I needn't have worried. Archie was curled up on my bed asleep and had most likely been there the entire day.

With a long stretch and arch of his back, he jumped down and headed downstairs, no doubt keen to greet Jackson, who had made himself comfortable on my sofa.

"Hey, Archie, how you doing, boy?" Jackson's voice drifted up the stairs.

Heading back downstairs, I passed through the living room to the kitchen. "Can I get you anything? Tea? Coffee? Are you hungry?"

"Actually, I'm starving," he admitted. "And I'd kill for a coffee."

"No need to go to those extremes. I'll fix you something. Sandwich okay?"

"Anything would be fine." He was fussing Archie who had climbed onto his lap and sprawled himself across Jackson's chest, his head resting under his chin. I could hear his purr from the kitchen. Turning on the coffee pot, I quickly whipped up a couple of sandwiches, wincing at the state of my refrigerator. I badly needed to do a grocery shop.

"Do you think I could borrow your phone?" Jackson called out.

"Oh. Sure." I'd forgotten someone had stolen his. Wiping my hands on my jeans, I dug around in my bag for my phone and carried it over to him.

Back in the kitchen I heard him talking, but his voice was low and I couldn't quite make out what he was saying. Not that it was any of my business, I scolded myself. I carried in a plate with two ham and cheese sandwiches and set it on the coffee table. Archie's head immediately swiveled, and his nose sniffed the air.

"Not for you," I warned, eyeballing my cat who'd

been known to steal food the second you took your eyes off it.

Meow, he complained, as if he hadn't been fed in days. I chuckled, heading back to the kitchen to get the coffees.

Curling up in an armchair, I nibbled on my sandwich, watching Jackson for any signs he wasn't feeling well. This was his first meal since his concussion and I remembered from experience the nausea that could ensue.

"Stop staring. I'm fine." He took a sip of his coffee.

"Sorry. I'm a worrier," I admitted, dropping my gaze. Then I had a thought. "Do you remember Remy, the girl I told you about in Australia?"

"The one who works for B.O.R.D?"

"Yeah, the Bureau. Well, Jenna's sort of been keeping in touch, since she and Mick are kinda dating."

"That's one hell of a long-distance relationship." He winced, and I thought of Jenna, how difficult it must be for her.

"Yeah. It's tough. I don't know how that will work long term. I mean, if it develops into something more... one of them will have to move."

"And you don't want it to be Jenna?" Jackson guessed.

I played with my coffee cup, turning it in my hands. "It's selfish of me to think like that." I sighed.

"But actually that's not what I wanted to talk about. Jenna has been doing her usual thing—"

"Investigating," he deadpanned. I nodded.

"She's been looking into the Griffin family, and let's face it, they seem to be at the crux of Emily's murder. Either Jacob did it, or he's being framed."

"That's a leap, but go on."

"She found a donation to Daniel's mayoral campaign from Richards, Jones & Tennant..."

"Ah, the law firm where your beau is a partner. So you're thinking? What? That Tennant paid him off?"

I ignored his dig that Blake was my beau. "What? No! No, while she followed that lead she discovered that Blake was here on other business, not just to represent Gran."

"And what business was that?" Leaning forward, Jackson placed his plate back on the coffee table, the sandwiches demolished. He'd definitely been hungry.

"That's just it. We don't know. But Remy said it was entirely possible he was on a clandestine case for the Bureau of Occult Research and Defense. Even though he doesn't openly work for them, his family has strong ties to the organization."

"And you're wondering if it's all tied in to Emily's murder?" He leaned back and absently stroked Archie's fur. The purring practically rattled the windows. Traitor cat.

I shrugged. "When I think of teenage pregnancy, I

think murder is an extreme reaction. Don't you?" I just couldn't get my head around Jacob, or even Hannah or Sarah, killing Emily. Yes, a baby was life changing, but bad enough to kill the expectant mother over? And so far I had nothing tying Ethan or Ryan to her death.

"There were no paranormal elements in Emily's death." Jackson was talking to himself more than me, but I listened intently regardless. "And as for her lineage, she was a hybrid, part witch, part human."

"Exactly. What if... what if the father of Emily's baby had a problem with their offspring being a half-breed? Or less than that if he himself was a hybrid."

"That rules out the Griffins, doesn't it? Jacob is a hybrid, his magic comes from his mom. So it wouldn't be like the baby was diluting the family line."

"Meaning his dad and his uncle are human."

"We're going around in circles." Jackson ran a hand through his hair, his brows pulling together in a frown. "We should get the results from the phone records soon—that may shed some light. In the meantime we need to find out who Tennant was investigating and why. B.O.R.D. doesn't launch an investigation willy nilly. They'd have good reason behind it."

"That's just it—Whitefall Cove Police weren't made aware, were they? Otherwise you'd have known about it, surely. Because you have jurisdiction here?"

"Not if it was clandestine, like you suggest. And

whoever he was investigating? Nothing came of it. Or nothing we know of," he amended.

A car pulled up outside, and I glanced out the window.

"That'll be Philips," Jackson said, rising from the sofa. "I asked him to drop off my laptop and a new phone."

I nodded, staying in my curled-up position in the armchair. Jackson greeted the young officer at the door, assured him he was fine and he'd be back on the clock in the morning but in the meantime to keep him updated with any new developments.

Settling back onto the sofa with his laptop open, Jackson was soon engrossed, his fingers occasionally picking out the keys as he typed in something. I soon became bored, flicking on the television, eventually dozing off to a daytime soap.

The harsh tone of my phone ringing woke me. Blindly reaching for it, I rubbed my eyes and peered at the screen. Jenna.

"Hey," I croaked, answering the call. It was dim in the living room; the sun was setting. How long had I been asleep? Jackson was sprawled on the sofa, laptop open on the coffee table, his dark lashes casting shadows on his cheeks. How he'd slept through my phone ringing I didn't know, but the steady rise and fall of his chest showed he was in a deep sleep. I frowned, wondering if I should be worried. Didn't they say you shouldn't sleep when you had a concussion? But the nurse hadn't said anything. Had she? She'd given a pamphlet to Jackson, but I hadn't even looked at it. I sat up, my neck cracking from the awkward position I'd fallen asleep in.

"I found out who made that donation to Griffin's mayoral campaign," Jenna said, reminding me she was still on the other end of the line.

"Oh?" Keeping my voice low, I eased myself out of the chair and headed upstairs so I wouldn't disturb Jackson.

"Yeah. Relax, it wasn't Blake. It was David Richards, one of the other partners."

"Oh." I wasn't sure if I should feel elated or deflated. Jenna plowed on, regardless. "Turns out one of Richards's favorite pastimes is getting involved in small town politics. He's supported several politicians in their efforts to gain power."

"Well, that's interesting, sure. But a dead end regarding Emily's murder."

Jenna sighed. "Pretty much. But I'm still looking into Blake. That man is too much of a mystery. I want to know who he was investigating."

"That's funny. Jackson and I were just talking about that this afternoon."

"How is he?" Jenna asked. I spent a few minutes filling her in on Jackson, and that Jacob Griffin had submitted to a DNA test.

A doorbell rang in the distance, interrupting us. "That's me. Gotta go. I'm covering the mayoral campaign and fundraising dinner tonight," Jenna said in a rush.

"Have a good time. Call me if anything interesting happens."

After saying our goodbyes, I hung up and headed back downstairs. Jackson was still on the sofa, but now his eyes were open. They zeroed in on me.

"Hey, you're awake." My eyes traveled over him. "Feeling okay?"

"I'm fine." He stretched, his shirt pulling taut across his chest.

"Sorry if I woke you." I was finding it exceedingly difficult to look away, mesmerized by the way the fabric of his shirt clung to his muscles.

"All good." He swung his legs to the floor and sat up. "Do you mind if I use your bathroom? I could use a shower to freshen up. I think I still have dried blood in my hair. Damn, I hope I didn't get any on your cushions." He turned to check, muttered under his breath in relief when there were no bloody stains.

"Go ahead. I'll fix us dinner. Towels are in the linen closet upstairs."

I watched him go, my eyes glued to his denim-clad rear as he climbed the stairs.

"I can feel you watching, Jones," he called down

and my cheeks heated with embarrassment until he added, "And I like it."

With a snort I turned my attention to the kitchen cupboards—empty. Followed by the fridge. Also empty. I'd used the last of the bread on the sandwiches. I had one slice of ham left and no cheese.

I *really* needed to grocery shop. I'd gotten spoiled living with Gran. The pantry was always full, as was the refrigerator, but now, living on my own, all of that was down to me. And I was failing!

Pulling out my phone, I ordered takeout. Again. While I waited for the pizza delivery, I fed Archie and cleaned away our plates and cups from lunch, forgetting that Jackson was using the shower so when I turned on the tap to wash the dishes a bellow coincided from upstairs and I quickly flicked the taps off again.

"Sorry!" I shouted, cringing at the icy blast Jackson had just received. I waited by the sink, gazing out the window and listening with half an ear for the shower to turn off. When it did, I quickly filled the sink with sudsy water and washed the dishes, leaving them to drain on the sink.

I heard Jackson on the staircase.

"Sorry about that. I forgot you were in the shower before I turned on the tap."

"Don't worry about it." He looked fresh, his hair wet and sticking up where he'd finger-combed it. His feet were bare and he dropped his shoes by the end of the sofa. He sniffed the air, then cocked an eyebrow at me.

"I'm not smelling anything cooking."

"Observant." I shoved my hands into my pockets. "I've ordered a pizza which should be here any second."

"Don't like to cook?"

I shrugged. "Nah, I don't mind it. Just lacking in ingredients right now."

"Ahh." He nodded sagely. Silence stretched between us and for the first time since meeting him, I felt awkward. That awkwardness was shattered when he burst out laughing. "You should see your face," he chortled, bending over and holding his middle. "Priceless!"

"What?" I grumbled, not enjoying being laughed at. He straightened up, took several moments to contain his mirth before reaching out to cup my cheek. "Relax, Harper. I'm not going to bite." He paused, sobering, his eyes darkening as he moved in closer. "Not without an invitation."

I swayed toward him, all thoughts of pique that he'd laughed at me forgotten. One thing that always was, and I imagined always would be, the magnetism between us was undeniable.

A sudden pounding at the door had us jumping apart. Archie meowed and trotted to the front door, waiting for someone to open it so he could greet whoever was on the other side. I'd been so engrossed in Jackson I hadn't heard anyone approach.

"That'll be the pizza," I squeaked, scuttling to the door and flinging it wide.

"One family-sized super supreme," the pimply-faced teenager announced. "A garlic bread, and a two-liter bottle of Coke."

I took the food from him and passed it back to Jackson who'd approached behind me. Archie wound his way through the teenager's ankles, sniffing him with interest.

"Hold on, I'll just get my purse." My purse was in my bag sitting on the hallway table by the front door. A quick stretch to my left, I pulled it free, paid the boy, and called Archie back inside. Closing the door I dropped my purse back in my bag and looked up, my breath hitching in my throat.

Jackson had never looked so darn sexy standing barefoot in my dining room holding a pizza. It would be a long night.

CHAPTER
FIFTEEN

I'd offered to take the sofa for the night, but Jackson had refused, insisting he'd be fine. I'd been half expecting him to join me upstairs, but he'd kissed me goodnight and whispered against my mouth he'd see me in the morning. He'd been a perfect gentleman, and I didn't know what to think about that. So I'd spent a fitful night tossing and turning knowing he was in my house, on my sofa, all I had to do was go to him.

In the morning I padded cautiously downstairs in my pajamas, careful not to wake him. I needn't have bothered. The sofa was empty. The pillow and blanket I'd given him neatly folded.

"Oh good, you're up." He greeted me from the dining room table where he sat with his laptop and a steaming cup of coffee. My nose sniffed the air appreciatively. "Coffee's on." He nodded toward the kitchen and I numbly followed my nose, pouring myself a cup before sliding into a chair opposite him.

"Good news," he said, his attention on the screen of his laptop, "Phone records are in for Emily."

"Oh?" I took a sip of the hot java, closing my eyes and savoring the caffeine hit.

"Mmmhmm. And she was exchanging a lot—and I mean a lot—of texts with someone."

"Hardly surprising," I mumbled. "She's a teenage girl."

"No, I mean someone who is not in her circle of friends." He flipped the screen around so I could see.

I looked at the spreadsheet with colored lines and frowned. "I don't know what any of that is."

Jackson swung the laptop back and grinned at me. "Not a morning person, I see."

I took another sip of coffee and eyeballed him over the rim of my cup. How could he look so bright and fresh after a night on my sofa? I'd had the luxurious comfort of my bed and I felt like a tired, drained, haggard, mess.

He studied me for another moment, seemed to weigh up his options, and opted to not mention my current state. Wise man.

"So we've extrapolated her calls—or texts—to her friends and family and have found one number that doesn't match up."

"Mrm." Another sip, keeping the cup raised and half hiding my face behind it.

"An unknown number. From a burner phone."

That caught my attention. My cup hit the table with a thud and coffee sloshed over the side. "Darn it." I cursed, beginning to rise to grab some paper towels.

"Sit. I'll take care of it." Jackson was up and in the kitchen in the blink of an eye, two seconds later he was mopping up the spilled coffee before tossing the soggy paper towels in the trash.

"Are you Superman?" I peered at him through bleary eyes. That was the only explanation I had for him moving so fast and being so refreshed. I knew he was a necromancer, but I thought that just meant he could see and communicate with ghosts. I hadn't considered he might have extra powers.

He laughed. "No. You didn't sleep well?" He cocked his head as he sat back down.

"Apparently you did." I didn't mean for it to sound so bitchy, but it did. I blushed and apologized. "Sorry."

He closed his laptop and studied me across the table. "Tell you what. Finish your coffee, get dressed, and I'll take you into town for breakfast. You weren't wrong when you said you had an ingredient problem. When was the last time you shopped?"

My face darkened and I could feel the heat in my cheeks, scorching. Pushing back my chair I went to stand up, but his fingers clamping around my wrist held me in place.

"Hey! That wasn't a criticism. Just an observation. I didn't mean to upset you."

I couldn't think of anything to say, just looked at him and he smiled, a soft tender smile that did funny things to my insides.

He let go of my wrist and nudged my coffee toward me. "Drink." Leaning back, he folded his arms across his chest.

"My sisters will like you." He nodded in apparent satisfaction.

My brows shot up. "You have sisters?"

"Yep. Three. Mae, Brooke, and Jasmine."

"Wow. That must have been fun, growing up with three girls." I took another mouthful of coffee, praying the caffeine would kick in soon and I'd stop acting like such a tool.

"Four if you count my mom."

"And yet you turned out so..."

"So?"

I coughed. "Manly."

He chuckled. "Thank you, Miss. Jones. But yes, I know all about living with a woman. I know when to bring her chocolate—or coffee—and when to leave her the hell alone. Mae is not a morning person. She's best not approached or engaged with until midday, at the earliest. But Jasmine? She starts the day bright eyed and full of pep. That irritates Mae no end." He grinned at the thought. "And Brooke is like me. We take the middle ground."

"What do your sisters do?" I asked.

"Mae is a funeral director." He ticked off on one finger, "Jasmine is a school teacher. And Brooke is an executive assistant at some big city firm."

"Wow... that's a diverse range of occupations."

"Isn't it though? They're all based in East Dondure. Mom and dad still live there."

"What made you move away from your family?"

He studied my face intently, his face somber. "I was shot."

I froze. Slowly I lowered my coffee to the table, so I didn't spill it again. "You were shot?" I repeated, eyes wide.

He nodded. "Me and my partner were ambushed. Got a call to a possible drug lab in the suburbs. We went to check it out. When we got there, they jumped us." His voice was rough, like he was chewing gravel. I reached across the table and clasped his hand. I had a bad feeling I knew what happened next.

He swallowed. "They left us for dead. I got hit first. In the leg. I went down, Bryan—my partner—landed on top of me. Winded me. They must've thought I was dead, covered in Bryan's blood, not moving."

"But Bryan? He was dead?" I whispered.

He nodded. "Hit in the chest and neck. No coming back from that."

"I'm so sorry." Tears welled in my eyes and I blinked hard, my vision swimming.

We were silent for a few seconds, then Jackson cleared his throat and shrugged his shoulders, as if physically shaking off the maudlin memories. "Lucky for me they didn't double tap me just to be sure. They ran. But my wound was a bad one, shattered my thighbone. I was bleeding out."

"You nearly... died?"

"I'd requested backup when we'd first arrived. Something had felt off. That was the only thing that saved me, those officers arriving when they did. Applied pressure to stem the bleeding, got me an ambulance. I spent weeks in the hospital after the surgery that pinned my bones back together, then months in rehab before I was back on duty. Only everywhere I looked, everywhere I went, reminded me of Bryan. I couldn't do it anymore."

"So you came here."

"So I came here." A deep breath escaped. "A fresh start."

"When was that? When did you arrive?" I'd been living in East Dondure myself at that point, I'd been there five years before moving back home.

"Just over two years ago."

"What does your family think? Having you move so far away after they nearly lost you?"

"You're very astute, do you know that?" he said.

"Why do you say that?" His answer surprised me.

"Because they thought I'd lost my mind. They thought I had PTSD, that I wasn't being rational."

"*Did* you have PTSD? Do you?"

He shook his head. "No. I have memories. The odd bad dream. Certain events can trigger a memory. Like hearing a car backfire can sound awfully like a gunshot. But part of my rehab was counseling, and I availed myself of it as much as I could. I joined the force to put the bad guys away, to get justice for victims. I didn't want that to change; I didn't want to become a bitter and twisted cop who turned up for work to further his own agenda. And I'd seen that happen too many times after an on-the-job incident. But despite all of that, I couldn't stay in the city."

"Did you see him? The ghost of your partner?"

"The little bastard was everywhere!" Jackson chuckled. "He hounded me."

"Why?"

"Because he got it into his air-filled brain I'd make a good replacement husband for his widow. Sam. Samantha. We'd all been friends, good friends, so when Bryan died..."

"Oh."

He nodded. "Exactly. Don't get me wrong, Sam is a

great girl, and I looked out for her after he died as best I could. But I wasn't in love with her, couldn't see that ever happening—and she felt the same way."

"So you left because of Bryan?"

"Partly. But also because I meant what I said. I needed a fresh start. Away from the hustle and bustle of the city. A quieter pace. My leg can give me trouble from time to time and, like it or not, I knew I had to slow my pace. Basically, I couldn't cut it in the city anymore."

I sat back in my chair, stunned—and full of sorrow —at his story. I'd had no idea. Those green eyes of his pinned me to my seat, and reproached, "Don't you be feeling sorry for me."

"I can't help it."

He grinned. "You've got a good heart, Harper Jones." He glanced at my empty coffee cup. "Go get dressed. It's time I got some food into you."

CHAPTER
SIXTEEN

Breakfast was at Bean Me Up, conveniently across the road from my bookstore. I hadn't opened at all yesterday and needed to make up for those lost sales today, so after breakfast I intended to hustle my butt across the road and open up. Shoveling fluffy pancakes drizzled in syrup into my mouth, I thought back on what Jackson had told me this morning about Emily's phone.

"How do you know it's a burner phone?" I asked, mouth full.

Jackson paused in devouring his omelet, studied me for a moment, then continued chewing. After he'd swallowed, he said, "Burner phones are basically prepaid cellphones with no information on who uses them, nor is there an owner listed for the number with the cellphone company. So while we can see that calls and texts have been exchanged with that number, we have no way of tying it to an actual person."

"So it could be anyone?"

"Yup. And I'd assume whoever it is would have dumped it by now, knowing we'd be looking at Emily's phone records. But we might get lucky."

"But it's still a breakthrough." I concentrated on cutting up a small portion of pancake and placed it onto a napkin, folding it up into a little parcel. "I promised Archie I'd bring him some pancake," I said, in response to Jackson's quizzical look.

"Ah." He nodded.

"But back to the phone. The kids all have their own cell phones. I'd doubt any of them had the finances to buy a separate pre-paid, or the smarts to realize they'd need one."

"Possibly, but we can't rule them out. Teenage psychopaths do exist, and the thing with psychopaths is that they hide it very, very well."

"Is that what you think? That Whitefall Cove has a psychopath on the loose?"

He shrugged, finished his omelet, and washed it down with a swig of coffee. A movement outside the window caught my attention. Jordan stopped outside the locked door of The Dusty Attic before spying me in the window of Bean Me Up. She waved and crossed the road to join us.

"Morning, Jordan, pull up a seat."

"Actually I thought, if it's okay with you, I could open up for you?" She bounced on her feet, her youthful energy exhausting.

"Sure." I dug my keys out of my bag and handed them to her. "I'll be over in a few minutes, okay?" Then I remembered. "I thought you might be rehearsing with Gran today, before tonight's big show?" Tonight was the talent show the town had been gearing up for.

"Yeah well, I'm not sure that's going ahead. And I lost a whole day's wages yesterday, so I'd rather be at work earning money."

"What? Why wouldn't it go ahead? What's happened?" I had heard none of this—why hadn't Gran told me?

"Some parents think it's best if we don't go ahead, that it would be disrespectful to Emily."

"Who? Last I heard everyone thought it would make a beautiful tribute to her if the show went on."

"Well, the Griffins mostly. I think they roped in Mr. and Mrs. Burton as well." Jordan jingled the keys. "I'm going to go open up. See you soon."

"See ya." I watched her leave, disappointed for Gran and the kids. They'd worked so hard, it would be a shame if they didn't get to perform.

Jackson reached out and rested his hand on mine. "I can understand why the Burtons might not want their daughter to take part."

I sighed. He was right. Hannah had been charged

with arson. I hadn't heard any gossip about it—yet—but word would get out soon. I nodded, unable to think of anything to say. It was a tough situation for the Burtons, that's for sure.

"Hey, Harper, Detective Ward." I glanced up to see Sarah and her mom, Kristin, standing by our table.

"How are you feeling, Sarah?" She looked good. Happy even. If I hadn't known otherwise, I'd never have thought she'd recently had an overdose. Okay, not exactly an overdose as it turned out.

"All good." She beamed at us, then Kristin spoke up. "I'm glad we bumped into you this morning, Detective."

"Oh?" Jackson looked from Kristin to Sarah and back again.

"Sarah's remembered something. From the night she was"—Kristin looked around then dropped her voice to a whisper—"drugged."

"Pull up a chair," Jackson said.

"I didn't really remember it. More like discovered it," Sarah said, dragging a chair from the neighboring table and squeezing in by my side.

"What did you discover?" Jackson used his cop voice and my heart skipped a beat. I loved him in cop mode. Dark. Intent. Sexy. It was all I could do to concentrate on the conversation at the table and not daydream about handcuffs.

"That night I got a text."

"From?"

"Jacob. Look." She pulled out her phone in its pink glitter case and handed it to Jackson. He studied the list of messages.

"Only, I didn't realize it was from Jacob at first, cos his number is in my phone so it comes up with his name, right? But this number didn't have a name, just a number I didn't recognize. But then I opened the message—well, see for yourself." She snatched the phone back, pulled up the message in question, and gave the phone back.

Jackson read aloud, "Hey, Sarah, it's Jacob. Got a new phone. Wanna hook up? Beach hut in an hour. Let's have some fun."

He looked up from the phone and our eyes collided. I raised my brows in silent question. Was it from the burner phone? He gave the slightest of nods. Whoever had killed Emily had lured Sarah to the beach. Posing as Jacob. Or it could have been Jacob himself. We couldn't rule that out.

"Do you remember meeting Jacob?" Jackson asked, passing the phone back.

She shrugged. "I think I vaguely remember getting the text. Like, now that I see it, it sort of jogs my memory, you know? Cos I was excited. I like Jacob and the text meant he liked me too."

I saw Kristin shake her head at her daughter's naivety. "That boy is a player," she said.

"He's not. God, Mom, you don't like any of my friends!" Sarah jumped up, all dramatic teenage angst and Kristin sighed in resignation, as if they'd played out this scenario a million times before. Probably had.

"Mind your manners, young lady," Kristen snapped. "You want me to take you shopping, don't you?"

Sarah forced a smile and through gritted teeth muttered, "Yes."

"Well then?"

Sarah looked from Jackson to me and said sullenly, "Sorry." And flounced off. Kristen returned the chairs they'd pulled up to our table to their rightful spots. "She's only gone and lost the damn hair ribbon I bought specifically to go with her dress for tonight." She sighed, shaking her head. "Insists we get another one, that the dozen other ribbons hanging over her dressing-table mirror simply won't do. Kids!" She squared her shoulders, plastered a tight smile on her face and bid us farewell as she hurried after her daughter.

"Would a hair ribbon—" I started to ask but Jackson's phone rang, cutting me off.

Glancing at the screen he said to me, "It's work." Then answered with a curt, "Ward."

While he listened to whoever was on the end of the line, I picked up the little package of pancake for Archie and stood, slinging my bag over my shoulder.

"That was the station," he said to me, finishing the call. "They've recovered my stolen phone."

"Oh? Where?"

He shot a look to a couple who had just taken the table next to us and I realized he didn't want to discuss it in public.

"Tell me later. We still on for tonight?" For despite everything that had happened over the last twenty-four hours, I hadn't forgotten that Jackson and I were scheduled for our first official date. My stomach clenched in anticipation.

"Wouldn't miss it," he growled, voice deep and low, sending shivers up my spine. I went to move past him, but as I drew level he whipped out a hand and wrapped it around the nape of my neck and kissed me. Long and hard. My knees gave out, and I leaned all my weight against him, feeling like a limp noodle only hotter.

Slowly he lifted his head, a mischievous grin on his face, and amongst hoots and hollers from the customers of Bean Me Up, he kissed me again. This time when he lifted his head it was to rest his forehead against mine. "I needed that," he whispered.

With my hormones in overdrive and legs so weak I could barely stand, I mumbled an inaudible reply and stumbled out of the cafe.

How I crossed the road without getting hit by a car I do not know. It was a good thing Jordan had opened up because I was reasonably sure I wouldn't have been able to control the trembling in my fingers long enough to get the key in the lock.

"Everything okay?" Jordan asked when I pushed through the door. "You look... flushed."

"All good," I squeaked, slinging my bag beneath the desk. I leaned against it, hand on my chest to settle my frantically beating heart. The chemistry between Jackson and me was undeniable.

"She just got kissed good and proper." Gran chortled, making me jump.

"Gran! I didn't know you were here. And how do you know that?" I blustered.

"I'm here cos you dropped Archie off this morning and asked me to bring him around once you'd opened the store. Remember? And I know that Jackson kissed you like every woman on this earth deserves to be kissed at least once in their lives because I saw— through the window."

"He kissed you? In public?" Jordan clasped her hands to her chest, a wistful expression crossing her face.

I cleared my throat. "Right. Yes."

Archie meowed and stretched up my leg, demanding the treat I'd promised him. Gran was right. I'd dropped him at her house on our way to the café since health code regulations forbade me bringing him inside. Unwrapping the napkin, I placed it on the floor, smiling as Archie purred in delight while scoffing down the morsels of pancake.

Now my mind was clearing I remembered what Jordan had told us at breakfast.

"Gran, what's this about the Griffins and Burtons wanting to cancel tonight?"

She huffed, flicked her hair over her shoulder, which would have been more effective if she had long hair—as it was the pixie cut she sported couldn't flick anywhere. "Not the whole show. Just our act." Her pout was unmistakable.

"Could you pull it off without them?" I asked. If Jacob and Hannah were to pull out that would leave four performers, Sarah, Ryan, Ethan, and Jordan.

Gran shrugged. "Maybe. Jordan partnered with Jacob, so she'd need to switch to Ethan and they haven't practiced together. They could probably do an okay job, but it would lessen our chances of winning."

"It's not all about winning, Gran."

"Pft, of course it is. But this one"—Gran winked at Jordan—"she's a quick learner. She can do anything she puts her mind to."

Jordan blushed, and I slung an arm around her shoulders and gave her a squeeze. "She is pretty amazing."

"Oh stop," Jordan half-heartedly protested. "You will give me a big head."

The bell over the door interrupted our bantering.

JANE HINCHEY

Who should walk in but Jeremy and Kathleen Griffin with their son Jacob? I glanced at Gran who'd folded her arms over her chest as if waiting for a showdown.

"Thought we'd find you here," Jeremy Griffin boomed. He was a big man, tall and wide with a belly hanging over his belt. "I want a word with you."

Jordan looked from the trio before us to Gran with huge round eyes. Sensing Jeremy Griffin was looking for a confrontation—and knowing Gran was more than capable of giving him one—I had to diffuse the situation, and fast. We had two minors witnessing the entire thing. This was not the type of influence we should have on our youth.

"Jeremy, Kathleen, wonderful to see you," I said, beaming, a fake smile plastered on my face. "You too, Jacob. All set for tonight? You guys are going to be amazing! I know Jordan's excited." Out the corner of my eye I saw her nod. "Have you seen their routine?" I asked Jacob's parents. "Your son is certainly talented. Not to mention he looks very handsome in his tuxedo."

"Oh." Jeremy sputtered, "Well... no... we haven't seen it."

"It's truly amazing!" I gushed. "To memorize the entire routine takes skill."

I heard Gran behind me and I waved my hand at her behind my back, warning her to keep her mouth

198

shut. If we played this right, we could get them on side, and I knew exactly how to do that. I hoped.

"Having his nephew win the talent competition would certainly help Daniel's mayoral campaign." It was my trump card. I had no idea if it would be effective, if Jeremy even cared that his brother was running for mayor, but it was all I had.

Jeremy looked to his wife, who shrugged. "She has a point," Kathleen said.

"A winner is better than a quitter," Gran piped up. I whipped around and mouthed "*Shut up!*"

The Griffins put their heads together and whispered amongst themselves. Jacob stood back, hands shoved in his pockets, an expression of utter boredom on his face. I studied the good-looking teenager and surmised Kristin was right. Jacob was a player. I didn't miss the way his eyes traveled over Jordan, resting on her chest for an obscene amount of time. I stepped in front of her, blocking his view.

His eyes shot to my face and an insolent grin twisted his lips while he dropped his gaze, blatantly staring at *my* bust. My palm itched with wanting to slap his face. Curling my fingers into a fist I sucked in a deep breath. What a conceited little twerp. He'd kept it well hidden, until now. I narrowed my eyes.

"Did you tell your parents about the beer?" I snapped, then immediately regretted letting him goad me. I wanted his parents to let him perform in the talent competition, not ground him.

Jeremy's head snapped up. "Yeah, yeah, we know all about it. Jacob is such a good boy, taking the blame for his friend."

"His friend?" I blinked in shock.

"Yes." Kathleen nodded. "Ethan should have known better. Really. But boys will be boys."

I almost exploded. This time it was Gran who shushed me, tugging sharply on my hair. I looked at her over my shoulder and she shook her head. Before I could say anything, Jeremy declared that Jacob could perform tonight after all and the trio exited the store, not before Jacob threw me an insolent wink on the way out.

SEVENTEEN

I had no time to reflect on Jacob or his parents, other than to mentally file away how similar he was in appearance to his uncle. It was uncanny. Jacob could easily pass as a younger version of Daniel; he was his uncle's doppelgänger.

But I had no time to ponder on that. A coachload of tourists swarmed the store, keeping us busy, wanting history books on the lighthouse and romantic novels to read on the beach. Thankfully Gran had hung around to help and Archie was in his element with so many people making a fuss over him.

After the tourists left, bags heavy with purchases, we had a steady stream of locals right up until lunchtime, when it quieted down. Gran headed off; she'd spied a tourist she'd liked the looks of and he said he was joining the tour group down on the beach for a pre-lunch dip.

"Make sure you take your bathing suit!" I called after her as she darted out the door.

"No promises!" I heard her shout as she hurried away.

"She wouldn't, would she?" Jordan turned to me, eyes wide. I gave her a reassuring smile but made no guarantees. With Gran, you just never knew.

The bell above the door jangled and Hannah stepped inside.

"Morning, Hannah, you here to see Jordan?" I asked.

"If that's okay?" Urgh, I wanted to hug this girl so tight. She was hurting so much and her parents couldn't drag themselves out of their own fog of grief to help her.

"Actually, Jordan, you can head off if you like. Go hang out, rest up for tonight. And—" I held my hand up so she couldn't interrupt. "Full pay. It's not fair you missed out on yesterday's wages."

"Are you sure?"

"Absolutely. Saturday afternoons are always quiet. I'll probably close up early, but for now I can manage on my own."

I made myself busy rearranging a display that had some empty spots after the swarm of tourists had descended. I liked that they'd bought so many books; it was a great problem to have.

I unashamedly listened while Jordan gathered her gear and told Hannah about the Griffins coming into the store earlier. Hannah rolled her eyes at Jacob's antics.

"Sounds about right."

"You two were an item once though." Jordan slung her backpack over one shoulder.

"That's what he told everyone, but it's not true." I remembered Hannah had told me the same thing. They'd gotten drunk and Jacob had told his buddies they'd slept together. Douche.

"I didn't realize how much Jacob looks like his uncle." I interrupted, steering the conversation away from Jacob's appalling treatment of Hannah. "I thought his looks came from his dad, but now I've seen them together I realize they come from his uncle."

"I guess." Jordan agreed while Hannah looked thoughtful.

"What is it?" I asked.

She tapped a finger to her chin. "I just thought of something. Something that makes it all make sense."

"What's that?"

"Emily. Going out with Jacob. I mean she's known him for years and had shown no interest whatsoever before. She once told me she likes older men, that the boys our age are too immature."

"What are you saying? That you think Emily was dating Jacob's uncle?" Jordan screwed up her face at the thought.

"What? No!" Hannah snorted. "No, I'm saying she went out with Jacob because he looked like his uncle. She's not going to go out with someone old enough to be her father, but she could fantasize that Jacob was his uncle. That would explain why I got the feeling she wasn't really all that into him."

Oh. My. God. Hannah was right, righter than she knew. What if Emily was having an affair with Daniel Griffin? What if he was the father of her child? He was running for mayor, a secret like this would ruin his career. At least Emily was seventeen and not under the age of consent, that could have landed him in jail. But still the age gap alone was enough to send the town into a tailspin.

Clamping my lips shut, I ushered the girls out of the store, promising I'd see them tonight at the performance. I closed the door behind them and leaned against it, heart pounding. It fit. Daniel would have the brains to use a burner phone, not to mention the disposable income to purchase one. Hannah said Emily had asked her to meet her at the beach that night because she had something to tell her. Maybe it

206

was about the affair and the baby. And Daniel turned up to stop her, only found her unconscious on the sand and took the opportunity to silence her once and for all.

But why attack Sarah?

Pulling out my phone, I dialed Jackson.

"Hey, babe," he answered. Babe! He'd called me babe. It was the first time he'd ever called me that and I was all a flutter. "Harper? You there?"

"Sorry." I cleared my throat. "Jackson, has Jacob's DNA test come back yet?"

"Not yet. Why?"

"I think the baby daddy is Daniel Griffin. It fits. Hannah just told me that Emily had a thing for older men—and Jacob is the spitting image of Daniel. I think Emily was going out with Jacob as a cover. And I saw Daniel at the beach the night of the fire, wearing a tie."

"Wearing a tie isn't a crime," Jackson pointed out. "And all of what you told me is purely circumstantial. We need evidence."

"We'll get that when the DNA comes in."

"That will prove if Jacob was or wasn't sleeping with Emily. And even then, it doesn't prove Daniel killed her."

"You're such a buzz kill," I muttered, hating that he was right.

He chuckled. "Just... don't do anything stupid, okay? Cornering a killer is never a wise move. Leave it to the professionals."

"Jackson Ward, I think you've forgotten who you're speaking to," I said in mock outrage.

His sigh was loud down the phone. "Please, for the love of God, be careful."

"I will." I blew him a kiss down the phone, then hung up. It immediately buzzed. Seeing Jenna's name, I swiped the screen, screeching into the phone, "I think I know who killed Emily!"

"You do? Who?"

"Daniel Griffin!" I glanced around, double-checking I was alone in the store. I was. But to keep it that way I flipped the sign to closed and locked the door.

"What are you going to do?" Jenna asked. "Confront him?"

"What? Heck no! I need proof. Proof I'll take to Jackson. If we can find the burner phone that Daniel used to communicate with Emily..."

"Burner phone?"

I filled her in on the latest news of the investigation.

"Are you thinking what I'm thinking?" I could hear the excitement in Jenna's voice.

"Probably not, but go ahead."

"We need to search Daniel's house. The phone has

to be there."

"Jackson will be pissed if he finds out." I hesitated.

Jenna snorted. "Errr, what is it you always tell me? It's easier to ask for forgiveness than it is for permission. It's not like that phone will be lying around for anyone to stumble across. We need to get into his house. Come on, not like you to wimp out."

"It could be dangerous—he killed Emily. Tried to kill Sarah." I felt it only fair to warn her we could potentially be walking into a killer's den.

"Has Sarah remembered anything?"

"Only that she got a text—a text she thought was from Jacob— asking her to meet up at the beach hut. Jackson says the text came from the same number as the burner phone."

"Sooooo." There was a moment's silence while Jenna mulled over what I'd told her. "Sarah goes to meet Jacob. But he doesn't show. Instead, his uncle turns up. She wouldn't feel threatened—she knows him—she'd feel safe."

"Exactly! And he'd already doctored the beer. So this time his actions are pre-meditated."

"But why try to kill Sarah?"

"Because he's worried Emily confided in her about the affair and the baby. I think killing Emily just happened. An opportunity presented itself and he made a split second decision. But then he didn't factor in Emily having two best friends she may have confided in."

"Do you think Hannah is in danger?" Jenna was following my train of thought.

"I'm not sure. He may have heard what she told the police—that Emily had wanted to tell her something but then she'd caught her lighting the fire and they'd fought. He may already know that Emily didn't have a chance to tell Hannah anything."

I could hear a rustling in the background. "What are you doing?" I asked.

"Looking out the window. I have the perfect view of the town hall—lots of activity today with the cleanup from last night and prep for tonight."

"And?"

"And I'm looking to see if mayoral candidate Daniel Griffin is in attendance. While I wait, let me tell you why I called."

I clapped a hand over my mouth. "I'm so sorry. I jumped right into my theory and didn't even say hello. I'm a bad friend."

"Yes. Yes, you are," she teased, chuckling. "So I've been working on trying to find out who it was that broke in here the other night. The balaclava-wearing bandit."

"I'd almost forgotten about that in all the excitement," I admitted. "Did they take anything?"

"Nope. Not sure what they were after, but it looks

like nothing was taken. But I managed to get some video footage from the security camera next door. They caught the intruder as he was leaving, conveniently carrying a black balaclava."

"Oh my God—who was it?"

"The weirdest thing. It was one of the fox's from the compound. Leon Johnson." The compound was a campground just outside of the town limits where fox shifters lived in a commune type setup.

"I don't know him. What's his deal?"

"That's just it, I have no clue. It's not like we've had any stories featuring any of them of late—they've been keeping a low profile."

"So what are you going to do? Go to the police?"

"I thought I'd chat with Jackson about it. I mean Leon was on the premises illegally, but he didn't damage anything or take anything—other than scaring the bejesus out of me." More rustling. "Ah-ha! I was right. He's here, schmoozing with his public."

"What?" I couldn't keep up.

"Daniel Griffin is at the town hall. Meaning now's our chance to search for that phone. I'm coming to get you. I'll be there in a few." The phone went dead before I could respond.

Gathering up my bag, I unlocked the door, glancing at Archie, who'd jumped down from the armchair where he'd been snoozing. "What do you think, Arch? Think you'd make a good lookout cat?" I couldn't leave him locked in the shop and I would not turn him out on the street.

Meow. "You're right. You'd make an excellent guard cat. Come on, let's go for a walk." Scooping him up, I let myself out of the shop to wait for Jenna outside.

CHAPTER
EIGHTEEN

I knew from experience that we could walk to Daniel's townhouse in a matter of minutes, deciding we'd be less conspicuous if we left my car at the back of the store rather than parked on the street outside of Daniel's place.

"Stop worrying," Jenna told me as we hurried down Main Street and swung to the right at the corner. "Just use your magic to hide us. It will be fine."

"Why didn't I think of that?"

"Because you are so used to *not* using your magic it doesn't occur to you to, you know, use it and make your life easier." We'd walked so fast I was puffing by the time we reached the gate to Daniel's townhouse. "Now would be a good time to weave some of that magic, Harper," Jenna hinted, cocking one hip as she waited impatiently.

"Oh. Right. Here, hold Archie." I shoved my cat at her, wiped my hands on my shorts, closed my eyes, then cast an invisibility spell over us. "Did it work?" I whispered.

"No idea," Jenna said dryly. "I guess we'll find out." She handed Archie back to me. "Now stand back and let me do *my* magic."

"You have magic?"

"I have fae skills. Close enough."

Pulling a clip from her hair she expertly picked the lock on the gate. Within seconds it swung open and my jaw fell open. I had no idea she had such hidden talents.

"I'm an investigative reporter. And sometimes a girl's gotta do what a girl's gotta do to get the story."

"I'm lost for words." Following her down the front path, I waited while she dealt with the front door lock.

"Uh oh." The door had sprung open silently and Jenna had stepped inside, I was close behind when she suddenly stopped and I ran into her.

"What?" I whispered.

"Alarm." She nodded at the keypad on the wall that was now flashing, showing that we had seconds to punch in the correct code before it alerted the entire neighborhood to our presence.

"Actually, I might have this. Shut the door," she said. I quietly shut the door and watched as she pulled out her phone, scrolled through the apps until she found the flashlight app and angled it toward the keypad. The light, shone on just the right angle, highlighted the four common keys pressed. We just had to get the right combination. She got it on the third try, with seconds to spare.

"Girl," Jenna grinned, "told you I had skills."

"You are amazing! Where did you learn that?"

"I saw it on TV." She nodded, proud of herself.

I turned, examining the room with my hands on hips. "We need to be quick. We've no idea how long Daniel will be gone. He could be back any minute."

Jenna slapped me on the rear. "Better get moving then, Jones." She grinned. "I'll take downstairs, you take up. Archie, keep an eye out."

I'd set Archie on the floor, but now he jumped up on a hallway table and dutifully sat, facing the front door. I couldn't contain my laugh. He looked so cute. Then I headed up the stairs, taking two at a time. Daniel had shown me the secret book he'd kept his spare keys in. If he had one hidey hole like that, I'd bet he had another. A perfect hiding place for a burner phone.

I went through the entire bookshelf, carefully pulling out each book, examining it for secret compartments before sliding it back. The minutes were slipping by and we'd barely scratched the surface.

"Ah, Harper?" Jenna said from behind me.

"Yeah?" I kept searching, not pausing in my task until I heard a strange noise. A click. Almost like... a gun being cocked? Straightening, I slowly turned, eyes widening at the scene before me. Daniel was back. And he had a gun against Jenna's head.

"Out," Daniel snapped, waving the gun to indicate I join them. I did. Slowly.

"How can you even see us?" I asked. "I cast an invisibility spell."

"I had a little witch cast her own spell over this house." He sounded smug, and I narrowed my eyes.

"Emily could spell cast?" I hadn't known that.

"Shut up and get over there!" He shoved Jenna toward me and waved the gun at us, ushering us over to the living room. "And don't even think of using magic to protect yourself. This house is warded to repel all magic."

Now that I'd gotten over the initial shock, adrenaline kicked in. I glanced at Jenna who was as calm and cool as a cucumber. I swear nothing rattled her. Standing by her side, a gun aimed at us, I reached my hand out and wrapped my fingers around hers. She squeezed, but neither of us took our eyes off Daniel.

"Now what?" Jenna asked. "You just going to shoot us here? If you do that, you'd better be prepared to run, long and hard. We'd be missed and there's no way the cops wouldn't pin it to you. Our DNA is all over this place, not to mention you'd have a hell of a time getting rid of the bloodstains. No little witch to help you anymore. Probably shouldn't have killed her."

I glanced at Jenna out of the corner of my eye. Was she crazy, goading him like that? She squeezed my fingers again, and I sucked in a slow deep breath, trying to calm my thundering heart. Then it clicked. She was buying time. The longer we kept him distracted the better our chances of catching him off guard and disarming him. I had no idea how—especially if my magic wouldn't work within these walls.

"Why did you kill Emily?" I asked. If I was going to die, I at least wanted to know why he'd done what he'd done.

"Actually, it wasn't me. I would have thought you'd have it all figured out by now. Miss Marple."

I narrowed my eyes. "You say it wasn't you? Yet here we stand, at gunpoint."

He huffed out a breath. "She was pregnant. With my kid."

"So you killed her? Bit extreme don't you think?" Jenna said.

"I told you, I didn't kill her. Had no plans to either. She refused to get rid of it so I'd arranged to meet with her that night for Plan B."

"Which was?"

"Send her to East Dondure to wait out the pregnancy, deliver the baby and put it up for adoption.

I'd arranged an apartment, private tutoring so her schooling wouldn't suffer. But the baby had to go, one way or another."

"Did Emily know you intended to ship her off? Force her to give up her baby?"

He shrugged. "Didn't get a chance to discuss it. I was running late, and when I turned up at the beach hut, she was gone. I figured she'd gotten tired of waiting and gone home."

"How do you know she hadn't already told her friends she was in a secret relationship with you? That she was pregnant? How long had it been going on, anyway?" I demanded.

"Long enough. Anyway, I took care of that."

"Oh?"

He waved the gun around as he spoke and I kept my eyes glued to it, worried he'd accidentally squeeze the trigger in his excitement.

"It pays to have connections in this town."

I rolled my eyes. Of course he had connections. I wondered if the council elections were rigged and if he was about to be made mayor via underhanded means.

"Do tell," Jenna drawled, her eyes drilling into him.

"You should know a businessman doesn't reveal his sources." He matched her tone. "Much like a reporter doesn't reveal hers."

"Let me think," I murmured. "How would you stop a seventeen-year-old girl from telling her friends about her secret boyfriend? There's not a lot you could threaten Emily with. Her parents are dead. What? You threatened to out her to her grandmother?" I pondered, tapping my chin. "But no, you'd be outing yourself. No, I don't believe you threatened Emily at all. But you were confident she wouldn't tell anyone about you—but not the baby."

I snapped my fingers. "Someone spelled her. Spelled her into not speaking about you, revealing your relationship. But then she got pregnant, and the spell didn't extend to the baby. And if she told people about the baby, they'd want to know who the father was—but she couldn't tell them—so they'd start digging. And you couldn't have that. If people found out, you could kiss the mayor's job goodbye, no matter how powerful your connections are."

The gun swung around, aimed at my head. I gulped. "You're getting quite the reputation, Ms. Jones," he said. "Too bad you never learned to keep your nose out of other people's business."

"Not my fault you did a crap job at getting rid of Emily's body," I snapped back. "If I hadn't found her on the beach I most likely wouldn't be involved at all. You only have yourself to blame."

His jaw clenched, he ground out, "I told you. I did not kill her."

Jenna cleared her throat. "Who did then?"

"That would be me." Sarah McClain stepped out

from behind Daniel. His big frame had hidden her approach. Only Daniel appeared as startled as we were. He swung around and she brought a baseball bat down on his arm. I winced at the crack it made as the wood connected with flesh and the gun dropped from his hand. With a howl of pain he cradled his arm to his chest.

"I think you broke it," he groaned.

"Don't care." Scooping up the gun she aimed it at Daniel. "Over there. With them."

I looked at Jenna in confusion. "What's happening?" I whispered.

"No clue," she whispered back, lips barely moving.

Daniel staggered to my side, his face pale. Tossing the baseball bat aside, Sarah trained the gun on us.

"Is it true?" Jenna asked. "Did you kill Emily?"

She cocked her head, slowly swung the gun to focus on Jenna, then shrugged.

"Guess it can't hurt to satisfy your curiosity. You will be dead soon too."

Jenna and I looked at each other then back at Sarah. I wasn't sure how we would get out of this one and was secretly hoping Jenna had come up with something while we were buying time.

"Emily was barely conscious when I found her. Jacob and I had planned to meet up at the beach hut, instead I found Emily, bleeding. So I helped her inside, initially I was going to call for help, but then I had a thought. Jacob wanted me. He just wanted to win the conquest of sleeping with Emily before he'd dump her, but she wouldn't give it up and it became more and more of a challenge for him."

"Oh God, I think I'm going to throw up." Daniel was as white as a sheet and I wasn't sure if it was from what Sarah was saying or the pain of his undoubtedly broken arm.

"Shut up," she barked at him. "I knew he didn't love her. She was just a conquest to him. So I figured, with her out of the way..."

"No, seriously. I'm gonna hurl." Daniel clamped a hand over his mouth.

"Nice try." Sarah sneered. "Back it up." She waved the gun at Daniel, but he stayed where he was, crouched over with a hand clamped to his face. Then he crumpled to the floor, out cold.

I blinked. Well. That was unexpected. Sarah cocked her head, nudged Daniel with her foot, then gave him a hard kick in the ribs just to be sure. Nothing. Shrugging she turned her attention back on us.

"Now, where was I?"

"You and Emily. In the hut," Jenna said.

Sarah nodded. "Right. I made a split second decision to use her head injury to my advantage. She was out of it anyway, didn't feel a thing as I choked her to death. Then I dragged her out into the ocean."

"Expecting the tide to take her away," Jenna cut in. "Only it didn't. It washed her back ashore."

"Didn't matter. She was still dead." She wiggled the gun. "Pick him up and put him on the sofa. Now! Move it!"

Hurrying forward, Jenna took one side, I took the other, and together we heaved Daniel onto the sofa. His head lolled back, and I pressed my fingers against his neck. Good. Nice strong pulse. Although for how long with Sarah waving that gun around was anyone's guess.

"You." She pointed the gun at Jenna. "Go into the bathroom and get a glass of water. And don't try anything. You do, and your friend here gets it." She stepped forward and pressed the barrel of the gun against my forehead. I closed my eyes and prayed.

"I'm not going to try anything," Jenna assured her. She was back in minutes with a glass of water.

"Now throw it on him," Sarah ordered.

Jenna did and Daniel woke with a start, wiping his face and cursing when he jostled his broken arm.

"What are you doing here, anyway?" he ground out, jaw clenched as he glared at Jenna.

"I imagine they were looking for the phone," Sarah said. "The one with all the evidence on it. God, what an idiot, not even deleting the texts."

"How do you know about it?" I asked, beyond curious.

"Uh duh." She rolled her eyes. "Emily told me."

"She told you?" Daniel sputtered, his face paling.

"Yes, genius. She did. Now shut up."

I looked at Jenna. This wasn't adding up. Emily couldn't have told Sarah about the phone; she was spelled not to talk about her relationship with Daniel, and the phone was how they communicated.

"Now what?" Jenna asked. "Are you going to shoot us?"

"Don't be silly, I'm not going to shoot you." Sarah laughed, an unhinged, creepy sound. "He is." I half expected Jacob to come strolling out, but instead she nodded toward Daniel.

"Now I'm really confused," I muttered.

"I know what she's up to," Jenna said. "She's going to frame Daniel for our murder. Just like she framed Jacob for Emily's. Am I right?"

"Stop talking!" she leveled the gun at Jenna's head. I held my breath, my heart pumping so hard I thought it would beat right out of my chest. I had an awful feeling we would die here today at the hands of a psychotic teenager.

And I still hadn't had my first date with Jackson.

CHAPTER
NINETEEN

"It's really rather clever when you think about it," Jenna said conversationally. "Who would suspect you when Jacob was the boyfriend and Daniel the lover? I mean, they're the obvious suspects. A love triangle. Only Jacob didn't really love Emily."

Sarah scoffed. "Of course he didn't. He went out with Emily because he wanted to get into her pants. But she wasn't putting out, and that irked him no end. That's why he turned to me."

"Turned to you? So, what? He was dating you? In secret?"

She tossed her hair over one shoulder and nodded. "We've had sex three times." She held up three fingers, as if immensely proud of it. "But he's a stupid boy who just wanted to nail Emily that one time, to brag about it to his buddies."

"Ahhh." I nodded. So part of what Jacob had told me was true. "He wouldn't break up with her. That must have hurt."

A dark flush crept up her neck and into her cheeks and the gun settled on me. I swallowed. Then she grinned. It was the most unnerving thing I'd ever seen. My stomach flip-flopped.

"You really are a psychopath." The way Jenna said it, so calmly, as if our lives weren't in immediate danger, had me turning my head to look at her. Her eyes met mine, then darted down, then back to me. What? What was she looking at?

"I wouldn't have thought so," Sarah replied. "But I'm discovering death is not as distasteful as I would have thought. And it's an excellent solution to one's problems."

Then I saw it, approaching behind Sarah's legs. Archie. He crept along on his belly, golden eyes now black, ears laid flat against his head. I focused my eyes back on Sarah, not wanting to give away the fact that my cat was stalking her. This could be the distraction we needed. I squeezed Jenna's hand, and she squeezed back. She'd seen Archie before I had. We just had to keep Sarah talking until Archie made his move.

"I'm curious though," I asked, turning my attention to Daniel, trying to keep my voice even, "what did you use to keep Emily quiet? Did another witch help you?"

He grimaced. "Hardly. If you want something done under the radar, who would you go to?"

"The foxes," Jenna said.

I looked at her in surprise. "What?"

She shrugged. "I've used them a time or two myself. Not for murder," she clarified, "but they are fantastic at getting information or certain items that are otherwise hard to get."

"Now I'm really confused," I admitted. "So foxes can spell cast?"

"Foxes are excellent herbalists," Jenna answered. "Isn't that right, Daniel?"

He nodded. "They are."

"So... no spell?"

He shook his head. "No spell. But a certain combination of herbs, a strand of my hair, a strand of Emily's, creates a special concoction that when consumed, bound her to silence. She couldn't talk about me. Ever. About anything. It's brilliant."

"Until she got pregnant. That was careless of you."

"An unfortunate accident." He lowered his head for a moment before jerking it back up and glaring at us. "I liked Emily. She had potential."

"Potential?"

"Once she was eighteen I'd intended to make our relationship public. I'd be mayor by then, and she only had her grandmother, so minimal family interference. She was an attractive young woman."

"Who you could mold into the perfect... what? Wife?"

"Eventually." I couldn't contain the eye roll. What an egotistical prick. I was busy fuming about it and almost missed Archie's big moment. Jenna squeezed my fingers, hard, just as Archie launched, an almighty leap from the floor to the top of Sarah's head, where he clung, claws extended, digging into Sarah's scalp and neck.

"Get the gun!" Jenna shouted, launching forward while Sarah danced around yelling and trying to dislodge Archie. I leaped into action, grabbing Sarah's wrist and wrestling the gun from her grip. Now I had it, I had no idea what to do with it. Staggering back out of reach, I held it in trembling hands and aimed it at Sarah's chest.

I needn't have worried. Sarah couldn't have cared less; she was more intent on getting an infuriated Archie off of her. Blood ran down her face where Archie's claws had dug deep. Jenna had her hands at Sarah's belt and I wondered what on earth she was doing until I saw her slide the belt free, grab one of Sarah's flailing fists and, creating a loop with the belt, slide it over and pull it tight around her wrist. Dragging that arm behind her back, Jenna maneuvered behind her, kicked her hard in the back of the knee so she collapsed to the floor, and with one arm incapacitated behind her, Sarah fell face first.

"Omph."

Archie leaped clear, running to my side. I crouched, gun now aimed at the floor, while I ran a reassuring hand over Archie.

"Help me with her," Jenna grunted, having trouble keeping Sarah pinned to the floor and capturing her free arm. Setting the gun down, I hurried forward, sitting on Sarah's back.

She groaned in protest. "Can't breathe," she gasped.

"Don't care," I shot back. Jenna captured the free arm and soon had it wound up with the belt and tied behind her back. She looked at me, face flushed and triumphant.

I smiled. "Time to call the cops?"

Her smile was wide. "Time to call the cops."

CHAPTER
TWENTY

We sat in the darkened town hall, eyes glued to the extravaganza taking place before us on the stage. Gran had outdone herself, stepping in at the last minute to take Sarah's spot, partnering with Jacob, and together with Hannah, Ryan, Ethan, and Jordan, flew through the air, spinning, swirling, performing dance moves from hip hop to ballroom, all seamlessly melded together.

Jackson threaded his fingers through mine and squeezed. I turned and smiled at him.

"They're fantastic," he whispered, leaning in close.

"They are." I nodded, feeling proud, both of the teenagers and Gran.

The dance ended on an explosion of glitter that rained down on the audience. I jumped to my feet, clapping, and everyone else followed suit. The students stood in a line on stage and held hands before bowing, low and deep. Jackson stuck his fingers in his mouth for an ear-splitting wolf whistle. Gran bowed with her students and the crowd roared. Shaking my head and chuckling, I cheered even louder. Finally, the noise settled, and we resumed our seats for the next act.

"I'm not sure anyone can top that," Jackson said, adjusting his long legs until his thigh was resting against mine. I liked the heat of it, and with no thought, rested my hand on his leg. He placed his hand over mine and that's how we sat for the rest of the show.

"Ladies and Gentlemen," Izzy Higginbottom said, striding out onto the stage, looking glamorous and elegant in a long, sparkling, gold dress, "I'm sure you'll join me in once again thanking all of our contestants in this evening's talent competition." We erupted in thunderous applause and cheering until she waved us into silence. "But alas, we can only have one winner. The poor judges had their work cut out for them this evening, from the dazzling aerobatic display of the Wicked Witches, to the sword swallowing endeavors of young Miles Brockhard, to the entertaining efforts of Whitefall Cove's own Houdini, plus so many more. I have the envelope here—can I have a drum roll, please?"

The orchestra below the stage obliged, a long and

loud drumroll followed by a clash of symbols, as Izzy opened the envelope.

"Starting at third place," she announced dramatically, "we have Donna the Dexterous!" Donna Columbine hurried onto the stage, still dressed in her leotard costume and accepted the trophy Izzy presented her with. She then moved to stand center stage and await the remaining two announcements.

"Second place goes to... Stephen Kemp for his incredible array of card tricks." Nine-year-old Stephen skipped onto the stage, the tails of his tuxedo fluttering behind him, his face beaming with pride. Izzy kissed his cheek and pretended to swoon. After Stephen had accepted his trophy and joined Donna, Izzy returned to the announcement we'd all been waiting for.

"And the winner of this year's Talent competition is.... the Wicked Witches!" Gran and her students burst onto the stage, doing cartwheels and somersaults. My eyes filled with tears I was so happy for them. It had been a tumultuous few days, but they'd persevered and I couldn't be prouder. I dabbed under my eyes with a tissue.

"Happy tears?" Jackson asked, breath hot in my ear.

I nodded. "Very happy tears."

The main lights came on and the audience started to file out. It had been a wonderful evening. With my hand in Jackson's, we headed down the center isle. We'd had no time to grab dinner as we'd intended to before the night's show, not with the arrest of Sarah. Now my stomach was growling.

"Shall we grab a table at Brewed Awakening?" Jackson asked, "They keep the kitchen open late."

"That sounds perfect. I'm starving." Jackson led me to his car with a hand on the small of my back, before helping me into the passenger seat.

"Your Gran did a fantastic job with the kids," he said, sliding behind the wheel. "Even if her dress was... unusual."

Gran had worn a black spandex body suit with a cage dress over the top, and a sparkling tiara perched on her head.

"She did, didn't she?" I agreed. "She said if they won she'd take them all for burgers and shakes at The Silent Bite."

He threw a glance at me. "I was surprised Jacob was there tonight, what with the arrest of his uncle."

"Same." I turned to face him. "I just can't believe Daniel Griffin had been carrying on a relationship with a teenager for all this time and no one knew! He told us he'd gotten some herbal concoction from the foxes that prevented Emily from telling anyone about him, but how they weren't spotted sneaking about is... amazing and appalling."

"What were you even thinking, going to his house,

Harper?" Jackson shook his head as he reversed the car.

"I told you, we were looking for the phone," I grumbled, crossing my arms over my chest. I knew he wouldn't be happy when he found out, and he hadn't been. When I'd called to say we were at Daniel's house and had performed a citizen's arrest, he'd been remarkably calm. When Jenna had handed over her phone, which, unbeknownst to me she'd used to record the entire confrontation with Sarah, getting her confession to killing Emily on record, and Daniel's involvement in the whole sordid affair, he'd gritted his teeth but remained calm. But now? Now I was waiting for him to erupt.

"You didn't have to do that. You should have left it to us."

"But you didn't know it was her!"

"Neither did you!"

"I had a hunch." It wasn't entirely true. My hunch was that Daniel was the killer.

"And I had a lead. A solid lead. We would have got her without you and Jenna putting yourselves at risk like that. We caught the guy who assaulted me and stole my phone."

"What? That's great, but what does that have to do with this?"

"Because the fox we arrested was all too happy to

spill the beans on what he knew for a reduced sentence."

"Wait! A fox? Who?"

"Leon Johnson. Do you know him?"

I shook my head. "No, not personally. But Daniel admitted that a fox helped him. And that name, Leon, that's who Jenna said had broken into the *Tribune* offices."

"Yeah, Griffin had paid him to plant a listening device in there, so he'd have a heads up if anyone picked up on his connection with Emily."

"Did Daniel have him attack you?"

Jackson shook his head. "Nope. That was all Leon. He hadn't planned it, saw me on the street outside your store, figured he owed me one since we arrested a fox recently, so he smacked me over the head with a rock, then panicked and didn't know what to do with me. He knew he couldn't take me out to the compound. So he broke into your store and left me there."

"Why did he steal your phone then?"

"To pawn it. Only the pawn shop wouldn't take it. No pawn shop will touch a police issue cell phone."

"So how did the police find it?"

"When Leon took it into the pawnshop, the owner turned it on. That's when they saw the Whitefall Cove Police emblem on the lock screen—knew it was police issue. Leon bolted, leaving it behind. And IT had been keeping an eye out for when it got switched on. A patrol car was there within minutes. The owner had been expecting them, had the CCTV footage of Leon bringing it in. Boom, busted."

"And then Leon dished the dirt on Daniel."

We'd arrived at Brewed Awakening and Jackson turned off the engine, turning to face me. "Daniel has been working with the foxes for years, using them to dig up dirt on other people on the town council, potential business deals, that sort of thing. Emily isn't the first young girl he's had a relationship with. Leah Spears was his first. Turns out he'd had a clandestine affair with her for three years, from sixteen to nineteen. Then he broke it off with her."

"But why didn't she say anything?"

"I'd imagine he dosed her with the same concoction he'd used on Emily. Only with Emily, he'd accidentally gotten her pregnant."

"So this herbal brew doesn't wear off? It's for life?"

"Undetermined. We've got a sample from Leon and sent it to the lab in town. Something like that is like a bad drug on the streets. We need a way to determine if anyone has been affected by it, and if they have an antidote."

"You think Leon could have supplied others?" I gasped. It was alarming to think what could happen.

"He swears he hasn't. The foxes frown upon using it. They won't be pleased when they hear Leon sold not one, but two batches to Griffin. When he gets out of jail they may banish him from the compound."

Jackson reached his arm along the back of the seat and played with my hair. "Promise me one thing, Harper."

"What's that?" I tilted my head to rest my cheek against his arm, loving the warmth of him.

"No more running into dangerous situations. In fact, no more sleuthing, I don't think my heart can take the stress."

"Okay." I grinned.

He frowned. "Really? Why don't I believe you?"

"No more sleuthing... today."

He threw back his head and laughed. "Knew that was too easy. Come on, let's go eat." He shot out of the car and was around opening my door in the blink of an eye. I tucked my hand through his elbow and we walked inside.

Monica greeted us. "Ah good, you're here. Everything is set."

"Everything is set?" I repeated, puzzled. What was going on here?

"Excellent. Thank you." Jackson smiled at her.

"Nothing is too good for my friend Harper." Monica grinned, then led us to a beautifully set table, complete with tablecloth, silverware, crystal glasses, candles and a single red rose. We were tucked away in a corner, dark and intimate.

"Oh, this is beautiful." I gasped, smiling in delight when Jackson held out the chair for me.

Monica poured champagne into two flutes, then bowed ever so slightly. "I'll be back to take your order in a minute." Then she was gone.

"Jackson," I breathed, "this is amazing! How did you organize this? There wasn't time."

"I was as disappointed as you that we couldn't keep our initial reservations, but I thought I'd take the chance I'd be free from work by, oh, about now, and called Monica, asked if she could help me out. She obliged. It's a step up from the usual, huh? This place rarely offers table service."

We clinked glasses, and I'd just taken a sip, the bubbles bursting on my tongue when my phone beeped. I automatically went to check it but then stopped myself. No. I was on a date. My first date with Jackson. The phone could wait.

I looked up to find him smiling at me, an indulgent expression on his face. "Go ahead. It could be your Gran."

"You don't mind?"

"Of course not. My job interrupts us constantly. I'm hardly in a position to complain if someone needs you."

Pulling out my phone I looked down to see a message from Jenna. I froze, hardly breathing as I read the words. I looked up at Jackson, in shock.

"What is it?" he asked, leaning across the table toward me. I held up the phone, and he squinted at the screen, reading the message.

"Well, I'll be damned," he muttered.

Jenna had found out who Blake Tennant had been secretly investigating. It was Jackson. Necromancers were banned in many communities for fear of inflicting flesh-decaying magic. B.O.R.D. had ordered Jackson be checked out to see if he had the ability.

"Suffice it to say, I don't." Jackson shrugged. "I'm a pretty boring, ghost-seeing necromancer."

"I didn't even know that was a thing," I admitted, slightly horrified that Blake had been investigating Jackson.

"It's always a worry with necromancers, that we may have the ability to raise an un-dead army."

"And what then? What if you had that ability?"

He gave me a tight smile. "You don't want to know. How about a change of topic, love?"

I studied him through narrowed eyes, wanting to take it further, but finally acknowledging he was right. Why get upset over something that hadn't happened? Jackson was fine. He'd been cleared.

"There's something about Emily's case that bugs me," I said, taking a sip of my champagne and dutifully changing the subject.

"What's that?"

"How did Sarah get the phone? How did she even know about it?"

"The night she found Emily injured, Emily had been delirious and had told Sarah to call Daniel on his secret phone."

"But I thought Emily couldn't talk about Daniel?"

"Seems the herbs weren't effective when she was in a concussed state." Jackson shrugged.

"So then what happened? I saw the text from the burner phone on Sarah's phone. How did she get Daniel to send it?"

"She didn't. She stole it. Sent the text to herself. She was at Daniel's house to return the phone—and frame him—when she stumbled upon the three of you."

"But Jacob—or Daniel—drugged her." I was still confused.

Jackson shook his head. "She staged the whole thing. Sarah stole the phone from Daniel's place, and one of the beers Jacob had stashed in his bag. She sent the text from the burner to her own phone, then turned it off and hid it in her room, intending to return it later. Then she swiped two of her mom's pills, climbed out the window and headed to the beach. She let herself into the beach hut, drank the beer, leaving the bottle there with her fingerprints and DNA and traces of the pills. When she started to feel drowsy, she moved from the hut out to the beach, lay down in the sand, just out of reach of high tide, knowing she'd be discovered before anything untoward could happen."

"And how did you discover all that? You said you had a lead?"

"I told you, IT were all over the phones, who was texting and calling Emily. We had a trace on the burner. As soon as it turned on, it pinged the closest tower. And that was not near Daniel's house. And because Sarah lived around the corner from Jacob, it was his house or hers. We were serving search warrants on both. Until I got your call."

"I'd thought for sure Daniel had strangled Emily with his tie." I sighed, hating that I'd gotten it wrong.

Jackson grinned. "I know you did. And to be fair, the fiber we pulled from Emily's neck had been blue, which was the same color as Daniel's tie, only the tie was silk and this fiber wasn't."

"What was it?"

"Satin. The same satin as Sarah's hair ribbons. We found the one we think she killed Emily with shoved in the back of a drawer in her bedroom. It had Sarah's and Emily's epithelial cells and the ME matched it up to the ligature marks on Emily's neck."

Jackson cocked his head and studied me across the table. "Any more questions?"

I shook my head. "Nope, I think I'm good."

"Excellent. In that case." He stood, came around to

my side of the table and held out his hand. I placed mine in it and allowed him to pull me to my feet.

"What's happening?" I whispered as he swung me into his arms and began to sway to the rhythm of the music pumping from the jukebox.

"We're dancing," he murmured, holding me close.

"So we are." I grinned, snuggled closer and closed my eyes, allowing myself to get lost in the music and comfort of Jackson's embrace.

"Just one more thing, Jones."

"Mmmm?" I lifted my head, and he kissed me.

Best date ever.

Ready to read Harper's next adventure in **Witch Way to Death & Destruction**? *Get your copy here:* www.JaneHinchey.com/DeathandDestruction

Thank you for reading! If you enjoyed this book, I'd greatly appreciate your review.

You can find a complete list of my books, including series and reading order on my website at:

www.JaneHinchey.com

Join my newsletter here:

www.JaneHinchey.com/subscribe

And finally, join my readers group on Facebook here:

www.JaneHinchey.com/LittleDevils

Thank you so much for taking a chance and reading my book . It's readers like you who make this journey worthwhile and fuel my passion for storytelling. Your support means the world to me, and I can't wait to share more exciting stories with you in the future.

xoxo
Jane

FREE BOOK OFFER

Want to get an email alert when a new book is released?

Sign up for my newsletter today, https://janehinchey.com/subscribe

and as a bonus, receive a FREE e-book of **Cupcakes & Curses!**

READ MORE BY JANE

Find them all at www.JaneHinchey.com/books

The Ghost Detective Mysteries

#1 Ghost Mortem

#2 Give up the Ghost

#3 The Ghost is Clear

#4 A Ghost of a Chance

#5 Here Ghost Nothing

#6 Who Ghost There?

#7 Wild Ghost Chase

#8 Easy Come, Easy Ghost

#9 Life Ghost On

Witch Way Paranormal Cozy Mystery Series

#1 Witch Way to Magic & Mayhem

#2 Witch Way to Romance & Ruin

#3 Witch Way Down Under

#4 Witch Way to Beauty & the Beach

#5 Witch Way to Death & Destruction

#6 Witch Way to Secrets & Sorcery

The Gravestone Mysteries

#1 Fur the Hex of it

#2 Battle of the Hexes

#3 What the Hex

The Midnight Chronicles

#1 One Minute to Midnight

#2 Two Minutes Past Midnight

#3 Third Strike of Midnight

Clean Scene Inc.

#1 All in Vein

PARANORMAL ROMANCE/URBAN FANTASY

The Awakening Trilogy

Hell's Angel Trilogy

The Enforcer Series (4 books)

Standalones

Returned

Secret Fates

Destiny's Touch

Blood Cursed

Heart of Darkness

ABOUT JANE

Hi there! I'm Jane, crafting tales of paranormal cozy mysteries sprinkled with urban fantasy romance. Between sips of coffee and dodging my mischievous cats, I immerse myself in stories where magic meets everyday life.

Once known as Zahra Stone in the world of steamy urban fantasy, I've now merged those fiery tales under the Jane Hinchey banner. Off the page you'll find me binging on true crime documentaries or sneaking in a Power Nap. Dive into my stories and join me on an enchanting journey!

Find me here: www.janehinchey.com

f facebook.com/janehincheyauthor

⊙ instagram.com/janehincheyauthor

a amazon.com/Jane-Hinchey/e/B0193449MI

BB bookbub.com/authors/jane-hinchey

g goodreads.com/jane_hinchey